A Week in the Life of

Amelia Nash

Sarah Healey

PORTLAND PRESS NOVELS

Published 2025
First Edition
Portland Press Novels
a New Haven Publishing Ltd Imprint
www.newhavenpublishingltd.com
newhavenpublishing@gmail.com

Cover design©Pete Cunliffe

PORTLAND
PRESS

ISBN: 978-1-915975-16-4

Sunday

They had told me she was dying, in a careful semaphore of telephone-authorised phrases: "very poorly", "not responding" and "massive stroke". It had all been happening, far away, before anyone found my number and called me, and by the time I arrived at the hospital it was Sunday night and all the doctors had gone home.

I was walking down a corridor, and when I got to the end I would have to go into the ward and see her. I didn't want to see her. Not that I didn't want to see her; I didn't want to see what had happened to her. Tubes and machines and death: the dark stuff that we spend our lives looking away from. I could say that my heart was pounding, or thumping, but it felt more like a faulty electrical connection, sparking and jolting as if it might pop out and leave me in darkness. Everything was so strange and unforeseen. I was her next of kin, her only kin. Marlowe Ward. I'd arrived. The moment had come. I had to go into the ward and see her. I pressed the intercom button.

"Hello?" The speaker crackled violently. The human voice was cheerful but brisk.

"Hello?" I leaned in and ran out of breath. "This is Amelia Nash's daughter. You rang me..."

"Come through." The speaker squawked again, and then the door buzzed urgently and I pushed into it. I had never before announced myself as Amelia Nash's daughter and it felt fraudulent, or at least in need of qualification and explanation, or even apology. My mother hated me; I had betrayed her; we hadn't seen each other for seventeen years. Yet now I was walking into the ward as Amelia Nash's daughter, wearing the face of her next of kin.

Beyond the double doors everything was fluorescent lights and beige plastic. There were broad windows presenting oblique views of large rooms, where high beds were lined up between pastel curtains. To my left was the nurses 'station, a thick chest-high counter, behind which staff skimmed back and forth, tapping at an old computer and holding rapid conversations. There were no windows to the outside: I had been plunged into a self-contained world of life and death, a world of disinfectant and needles and swabs, enclosed in pale yellow walls. My hands felt hot and cold. Then a nurse snapped into view in front of me and smiled.

"Miss Nash? Let me take you in to see your mother. The staff nurse will be available to talk to you in just a minute."

She propelled me without touching, and we were striding down another corridor. I was saying something vague, nervously; and then I saw on the wall a whiteboard where names were scribbled in impermanent black ink beside bed numbers. 'Nash' was written with a big bold capital 'N 'and a quick squiggle representing the other three letters. She was here, really here. Her name was on the board.

The nurse pushed open the swing door and we walked into the room, where there were four beds with four sick people lying down. I didn't know which way to look and was for a moment frightened I wouldn't recognise her. Then I saw her. Her eyes were open.

"Here, I'll pull you a chair round," the nurse was saying.

Her eyes were open, but they were fixed and unseeing, and she was snoring like an animal, her breathing fast and coarse. There was a machine with a monitor and a little tube coiling out of her wrist, but there were no fat tubes or wires or masks on her face. She was wearing a pink nightdress that definitely wasn't her own. She would never have worn a nightdress like that - "a granny nightie," she would have laughed, "bloody hell, me, in a lacy pink granny nightie" - so it must have been a spare, unowned nightdress the hospital provided. A nightdress worn over and over by the unclaimed people who came in without family or friends.

"I'll get the staff nurse to speak to you." The nurse left, and the door closed softly.

4

I sat down on the chair, a brown plastic school-assembly type of chair, and looked at my mother. Her blank eyes were uncanny. Her rough breathing sounded like she needed to cough. She was slightly raised up, lying tilted on a lump of pillows, a person unable to move herself, even to shift a bit, or cough, or blink. It was terrifying. I didn't know what I was supposed to do now - should I speak? Was I supposed to just look at her? Just sit here?

As I was driving to the hospital I had been trying to work out when I had last seen her, mentally thumbing through the past and remembering that day we met for lunch. Seventeen years ago.

"How are you?" I'd asked her, once we'd sat down at a table.

"I'm doing fine without you, thank you," she replied, in a challenging tone, and sniffed haughtily, not meeting my eyes. She was wearing an odd green leather coat and I felt slightly embarrassed about her. I'd been afraid she would look like a bag lady, but she was, as usual, unclassifiable: her make-up was neat but her fingernails were dirty. She swept her hair back from her face with her sunglasses, exposing the colour of her roots. I'd forgotten just what a presence she had; she occupied the whole cafe and no-one in the room could have been unaware of her. "Excuse me..." she addressed the woman at the next table. "Could we borrow your menu?" As she sat back to consider the laminated sheet she looked like an elegant lady, stroking her lips with a long delicate finger; then, within minutes, she was an obstreperous, coarse woman, an unlit cigarette provocatively spiked between her bony white fingers as she muttered "Can't bloody smoke anywhere these days," and flashed her head from side to side belligerently; and then, for just a moment, she looked like a mad person, a person that other people avoid looking at in the street.

When the waitress brought the food she was charming. "Oh, this looks lovely, thank you... ooh, I love your ring. Is it amethyst?" The young waitress smiled and submitted her hand, which my mother clasped greedily and raised to her eyes. To me, she was all claws and teeth, but the waitress saw nothing, and took back her hand, still smiling.

5

"Miss Nash?" It was the staff nurse, round and pink, tucking a pen into her pocket. "Would you like to come somewhere we can talk privately?"

I escaped from the brown plastic chair and followed her out of the room and back along the corridor, where she stopped and unlocked a door. She apologised for the state of the office and wheeled round a desk chair for me to sit on. There were box files stuffed into the shelves above the archaic, grey computer, and there was paperwork scattered about the desk. I felt as if I had been brought behind the scenes. She sat on the other chair, our knees close together, and explained apologetically about it being a Sunday night and the doctor not being available to speak to me until the next morning. She wore short sleeves and a tight silver watch, and on her wrist was a tattoo of a butterfly in rich red and turquoise. It was a beautiful image, but static; the opposite of a butterfly, it was flat and still, embedded in the woman's arm.

She explained that there are two kinds of stroke. One is a blockage: a clot gets stuck in a vessel and part of the brain is starved of blood, and dies. I pictured a brain drying up and curling like a riverbed in a drought. The other, the kind that happened to my mother, is a burst vessel, where blood rushes out, smothering the brain and killing it. A tsunami. She said that my mother had been alone, unconscious, for a long time before being found, and by the time an ambulance brought her to the hospital it was too late for the doctors to do anything. She looked at me closely as she explained this, and I realised suddenly that she was afraid I would be angry. She didn't know that my mother hated me, or that I had betrayed her, and while the nurse was nervous that I would blame the doctors for not doing more, I was nervous that the nurse would blame me for not being there when the stroke happened. We edged carefully around each other, self-conscious and guilty in the face of the enormous thing that had happened.

"She's only sixty," I was saying.

"Sometimes that's the way of it: sometimes younger people have more devastating strokes than those in their eighties. It might have been that your mother always had a weakness in a blood vessel."

6

We both seemed satisfied with that, the inevitability that it brought to the event - a weak spot in her brain that had always been there - no-one could have done anything. We were all absolved.

"Your mother's still breathing," continued the nurse, "because the spreading bleed hasn't quite reached the part of the brain near the spine, which controls the automatic functions, breathing and heartbeat." She gestured with her hands, explaining, as if she had an invisible brain in front of her. I pictured a grey, disembodied brain, trailing a spinal cord, and although I knew brain anatomy was complicated and mysterious, I imagined dark blood slowly seeping down through the higher thoughts at the top, the senses and emotions in the middle, and eventually into the animal functions at the bottom. "The bleed might still be spreading, we don't know. The doctor will be able to tell you more tomorrow morning."

"Might she die tonight?"

It was such a big, blunt question that it seemed to give me away: did I want her to die tonight? Was I afraid she wouldn't die tonight?

"We don't know." The nurse lifted her hands and again conjured the invisible brain. "If the bleed puts pressure on the medulla, her heart could stop at any time."

She dropped her hands and clasped them in her lap, the butterfly twisting awkwardly in the flesh of her wrist.

"Do you have any more questions?"

She was efficient but solicitous, just as I am when I'm at work. I was on the receiving end of professional sympathy. It was comforting to imagine myself in her chair; for her, this was an ordinary working day. The crumpled office we sat in was very like the office I sat in at work: the slipping paperwork, the post-it notes on the computer monitor, the noticeboard layered with forgotten notices and the furniture packed impossibly into the awkward, malproportioned space. It was a familiar place even though I had never been there before.

I work as an usher in a magistrates 'court. We have a small, leftover back room to hang our gowns and eat our sandwiches, and we perch on a cabinet corner to sort through courtroom listings and check names. Our fingers peck at the keyboard of the recalcitrant

7

computer and we complain to each other about the cumbersome procedures and slow software. We emerge from there in our long black gowns to enter the public areas, sombre-faced, and we usher: whispered messages in courtrooms, documents whisked away, names called. We find the fearful faces of the defendants in the waiting area and we lead them to the courtroom, holding open the door and stepping aside for them to enter.

The nurse had finished speaking and I had nothing to say. She showed me out of the office and I was back on the outside again, a bewildered member of the public.

"You don't need to worry about visiting hours," she was saying. "You can stay as long as you like." She was walking a little too quickly for me. "Let me get you a more comfortable chair."

She put me back at my mother's bedside. While I stood and waited, she scraped away my plastic chair and positioned a padded, high-backed armchair where I was to sit.

"Her breathing's so fast," I said. I suppose I was surprised that it wasn't the calm breathing of a sleeper. She sounded uncomfortable.

"Yes," said the nurse, but didn't elaborate. She took a little pink stick from a bag on the bedside table. It looked like a lollipop, with a sticky pink head, and she brushed it quickly and expertly over and under my mother's lips. "This is to keep her mouth moist," she explained, and then she looked directly at me and smiled. "Talk to her. She might be able to hear you, we don't know. Some people think hearing is the last sense to be lost."

"Oh...." I didn't want the nurse to go, but she was going. I was left sitting in my high backed chair with an expectation that I had something to say.

"Hello, Mum."

"I'm here, Mum."

"I'm sorry..."

"I'm sorry for all the stuff between us, Mum, but I'm here now."

"I don't know if you can hear me."

"I'm here."

"I love you, Mum."

8

I was speaking aloud, into the air, in this open place. I could see across to the next bed, where a very small, very old woman lay with her eyes closed. On her bedside table a flock of Get Well Soon cards clustered around a plastic jug of purple juice. A clear tube curved out from beneath her bedcovers to a thick plastic bag of urine clipped into a stand under the bed.

I looked at my mother and I didn't believe that she could hear me. That was wishful thinking, a panacea for those who were desperate to connect with their loved ones and couldn't accept it was too late. No-one could prove that they didn't hear those goodbye messages, the important things that they couldn't remember saying and the apologies for the things they could remember saying. When someone is half-gone, still breathing but gone, their thoughts and feelings are no more or less than what we imagine them to be, and it is our right as relatives to impose an intimacy onto the silence.

Of course, it might have been wishful thinking on my part, wishful thinking that she couldn't hear my silences, my awkwardness, my insincerity. What could I say? Stuff had happened. I loved her, she hated me. Or I hated her and she loved me; who can say which?

She looked pale, without make-up, her face naked and raw. Her hair was greasy and combed into a strange parting by a stranger. She looked very old, older than I would have expected, but that might have been because she was in a hospital bed; we all look ugly when we're helpless. I felt that I should touch her hand but I couldn't: it looked cold and yellow, as if her extremities were already dead; and in any case I hadn't touched her for so many years. When we lived in Willow House we had to share a bed, and I remembered the warm, safe feeling of sleeping back to back with her, heating each other, our shared warmth radiating like a pocket of home in that unfriendly house. Willow House was one of our temporary addresses, after the fire, when my mother was passionate and bitter. She was my protector back then, or so it seemed. I was eleven years old, and at school we were studying the Romans and the Praetorian Guard, the elite force that both

9

protected and controlled emperors. At that time I believed that my mother stood like a mighty centurion between me and the world.

The lights in the ward had been dimmed for sleeping, emphasising my special dispensation to stay outside visiting hours. Someone in the bed behind me was making a quiet keening noise, and after a while a nurse came in and drew the curtain around the bed. Indistinct sounds came from behind the curtain, and then the nurse left, softly. I sat in silence. I was reminded again of the Praetorian Guard: my special dispensation to stay and my high backed throne were nothing less than a prison, a requirement that I sit here, dutifully. Was I expected to stay all night?

For a long time nothing happened. My mother snored mechanically. The monitor beside her bed displayed three layers of jerking lines and numbers, but as I watched them they made no patterns that I could discern, and nothing synchronised with my mother's breathing, or corresponded to a heartbeat. I wasn't sure what other aspects of an unconscious human's output could be turned into numbers. I remembered learning, years ago, about the mechanics of the human body: the many millions of cells, each one a tiny independent machine; so many chemical reactions and electrical signals, such a complicated sequence of requirements just to stay alive, a system so impossibly delicate that thinking about it I almost forgot to breathe. Just being alive was so improbable. And yet my mother was dying so slowly, the systems continuing autonomously, without food, water or consciousness, ticking over, running on. Not really dying at all.

I remembered, too, that the cells of the body are continuously renewed, the tiny machines scrapped and replaced, so that nothing original remains of the person who was born. A human being is like the hammer in the old joke: two new heads and three new handles, but still the same hammer. But a human changes more gradually and continuously than a hammer: a person is more like a river, the water molecules constantly changing, the silt continually shifted by experience and time. The banks grow and shrink, the bends lengthen and shorten, but the identity of the river remains. Continuity and change, without contradiction.

10

My mother changed, perhaps more than most people. She wore different costumes. The fierce protector who slept beside me in Willow House was very different from the woman a few years later, in New Gaia, who braided her hair and fed chickens. She was never still, always trying on different lifestyles and transcribing different people. Perhaps she was trying to squeeze as much life out of life as she could. "Never boring, eh?" she used to say, when we crashed out of one place, or washed up at another. Or perhaps she was just never happy with who she was.

There was the sound of someone being sick inside the curtain behind me, and nursing staff, or perhaps cleaners, came and went quietly with sighs and scrapes. I could hear a nurse's voice, gently encouraging, but I couldn't make out the words. I couldn't look around the back of my chair. Was I supposed to stay here all night?

I became aware that I was wearing inappropriate clothes. All my clothes were inappropriate for this vigil: my clothes were casual and cheerful, not serious enough for the presence of death. I was wearing skinny jeans, bouncy white trainers and a pink sweatshirt with 'California' emblazoned on it in red. All my weekend clothes are childish and cutesy. Perhaps I dress to keep the real world out, like those grown women who fill their bedrooms with stuffed toys. My work clothes are black, of course, but work is a world apart, a realm of judgement as separate as Mount Olympus or Asgard, and I would never wear those clothes in any other reality.

I sat in the darkened room in my lighthearted clothes, and watched my mother breathing. This night was so strange and unforeseen.

"You know I love you," she said to me once. "You know I'd top myself if I didn't have you, you know that, don't you?"

There was a heap of stuff between us, a big slippery rubbish tip of things said and unsaid. But it was all over now, meaningless.

I sat for a long time looking at the monitor as if it were a puzzle, following the peaks and dips of the lines and the uneven sequence of numbers until I realised my mouth was open.

I was tired, and it was very late; in fact, it was Monday now, well into Monday, nearly time for early alarm clocks and the first buses, and I wondered whether I should go home. I wanted a kindly nurse to come over and say "Ooh, are you still here, love? You should get yourself home, get some sleep." But everyone was leaving me to take responsibility for my own grief. Adults are supposed to know about these things, and rise to the occasion. How could I sleep; how could I do everyday things like sleeping, eating or going to the loo when death was happening? I was here to witness mortality.

No-one saw me leave. I just got up and walked out of the ward.

The roads were vacant, but the traffic lights still danced through their routine. Accelerating out of the city, I left the streetlamps behind and drove the unexpected twists of the main road in an island of full beam. It was still dark but there was a gentle hum of dawn moving near. After a while I reached the outskirts of my home town, the road gradually joined by tributaries and accumulating traffic signals and signs.

I love my old car, from its choppy gear stick to its rust-rimmed rear window. It coughs a little in the rain. Driving it feels as comfortable as walking, like walking under a big umbrella, in a pocket of warmth and safety. The back seat is stocked with wellies and tissues and probably-out-of-date sun cream, and in the glove box I can rummage for CDs and paracetamol.

The sky was lighter when I arrived home. I couldn't remember ever being awake at dawn before: I've never been a party girl. A summer dawn, I mean, not a winter dawn, those creeping mornings when everyone crawls to work in half-light. A summer dawn is big and empty and unobserved. Then I remembered: when we left Willow House it was dawn, confusingly early, our stuff packed into holdalls and carrier bags. The house was cold and grey, everything silent and strange as if I were looking at it through a mirror. We were picked up by someone - Dave? Simon? - and I had to climb between the front seats to get into the back of the car, which smelled of dogs.

I read somewhere that our whole lives are actually stored inside our heads: we record everything, but we can only access our memories, which are feeble fragments that fall randomly within reach. Somewhere in my head there was probably a complete inventory of Willow House, from the flaking paint on the front door to the stains on the carpet, but my memory could find only vivid, unconnected glimpses: the heavy chest of drawers, its dark varnish scored by someone called Kieron; the pink bath scoured in a spiral around the plughole; the black mould that freckled the bathroom ceiling. My memory of the bed was not visual, but rather a feeling of soft, sinking depth, and the communal room I remembered only as a space inside which there was tension, edgy conversation and fights. There were other people living in the house, but some of them didn't stay for long, and in trying to remember them I found my recollections were mediated by my mother's commentary: "that old drunk at the top", "that Jasmine woman" or "the coffee thief".

I thought then of my mother's head, resting on the hospital pillow, slowly filling up with blood, like treacle gently rolling out, erasing all the memories stored there.

Monday

My parents split up when I was nine. My memories of our time as a family are vague and contradictory, mostly disconnected images of dinners, bedtimes and arguments, but in later years both my parents separately loved to tell stories of the golden age when they were in love, between the moment when they first met and the moment when I was born.

"He had this classic Mini Cooper, a tiny thing; I swear it broke down every time we went out in it but we didn't care. We'd set off to the coast and never make it, end up in a village pub..."

"...she was so full of life, you never knew what she was going to do next. We went to Ibiza - this was the late eighties, when Ibiza was cool, not tacky - we went clubbing all night and lay on the beach watching the sun come up..."

"...we went to raves, in the middle of nowhere; I remember one time this muddy field full of cows and two guys with enormous speakers in wheelbarrows..."

"...you've got to remember there were no mobile phones then, no internet, you just heard on the grapevine there was a rave and you all piled into a car and went to find it. One time your mother just got out of the car in a layby, pitch black it was, and she just danced, no music, just dancing around and laughing..."

"...we drank so much, and took speed as well - I don't know how we ever made it into work; we must have been off our faces..."

"...it was a wild time. Your mother, you know what she's like, like a whirlwind..."

"...I suppose I must have loved him then..."

"...she couldn't handle real life, adult life, being a grown up; I mean, she was twenty-five when you were born, it was time to grow up..."

14

"...he couldn't handle real life, though, the darker side of things; when I suffered from depression he said I should get a hobby. 'Let's have a Chinese tonight, 'he'd say, as if everything could be kissed better with a bloody takeaway. He's a superficial man, no depth to him..."

"...she got bored with everything. She sulked when life got ordinary. A video and a takeaway wasn't enough for her..."

"...look at him now, with his cutout wife and his cutout children. He's so fucking dull. So fucking ordinary."

When they split, Dad moved out of the house and for a while he paid the mortgage, but when he met Kate he wanted to settle up and move on, so we had to sell the house. Mum had a plan to stop him. "House viewing on Tuesday!" she would shout upstairs as she put down the telephone. "Action stations!" We would hang wet washing on the radiators, and boil four pans of water on the hob, bubbling away mischievously, steaming up the windows and walls." Is it feeling damp yet?" she'd say, and I'd breathe in, maybe touch the wallpaper, and grin. "More mess!" she'd cry, tossing clothes from the laundry basket onto the floor. "Untidy your room!" We would fool the prospective purchasers and the lady in high heels from the estate agency with our tricks, the opposite of the tricks suggested in the TV shows about how to sell your house by baking bread and arranging flowers. The loveliness of our house was our secret, and hiding it from potential buyers made it even more lovely to us. "Put that window ajar," my mother said, "so it looks like it doesn't close properly." She was busy, so fired up with purpose she was sparking. "Let's make some smells..." We giggled over our cauldron, cooking fish and cabbage, grilling cheap burgers and leaving fat and ketchup on the plates beside the sink.

Windy weather brought down a fence panel in the garden, and the next night Mum woke me with a torch. "Another terrible storm, eh?" she winked. Outside it was dark and shivery and exciting. I wore a duffel coat over my nightshirt and shoes without socks, and the grass was wet, tickling my bare ankles. We hadn't mown the lawn in months and it had rebelled in tangled clumps, sprouting tough-stemmed dandelions. I crunched an invisible snail under my shoe. Mum, in a long coat and soaked slippers, kept the torch low, and above us the sky was dark grey and glistening. She had a hammer. "Let's get the whole bloody thing down," she hissed, and set to hacking the edges of the slatted fence panels. My job was just to be there with her, shivering and giggling in the long wet grass. The next day we had a new vista: our garden opened into next door's and I could walk to the edge of a wide new space, neatly kept, with a greenhouse at one end. I was now overlooked by strange windows. I retreated back into the house, unable to play now that our garden was no longer our garden.

Mr O'Brien from next door came round. "Oh, I know, Frank," said Mum, in her dressing gown at the door. "It was dreadful weather. Wrecked the whole fence. I'll get it fixed as soon as I've got the money. I mean, David's supposed to be paying towards these things but, well, you know..." When people came round to view the house, she was ready with her story. "Yes, the fence," she said, pulling a face." I'm afraid we've had trouble with the chap next door. Any fence we put up gets mysteriously smashed. He goes on about not getting enough light in his garden. Quite aggressive." She drew back from the window. "Anyway, let's go upstairs. Mind the carpet, it slips a bit."

I can still remember my bedroom in that house. The window printed a trapezium of sunlight onto the wall opposite the bed and during long summer afternoons it slowly melted into a flattened rectangle. On Saturday mornings, luxuriating with a lie-in, I could hear wood pigeons on the roof. The carpet was soft and cream and the pile could be stroked and made to stick up in places; I used to lie on it, on my tummy, to do colouring in with my rainbow of felt-tip pens. You can pack a place away inside you, and carry it with you, just as it was: the place you leave behind becomes somewhere else, someone else's room, redecorated and refurnished, a different place entirely, but my bedroom still exists, in my head, where I packed it away. It's better there, actually. I mean, if I had carried on living there it would have changed, gradually, and it would have been lost, written over. Because I had to leave that room, it was forever preserved.

On Sunday night the hospital had been like the end of the world, a place of the dying and the desperate, a place of hushed

16

lights and low voices, grilles up at the shop and one weary man on the front desk. On Monday morning it was more like a shopping centre. The car park was my first shock: already, by nine, a queue of cars reached back to the main road, where southbound visitors sat in the middle with their indicators blinking, waiting for northbound commuters to do the right thing and flash them through. The car park was filling neatly, space by space, as the cars took their turns at the ticket machine and the flimsy wooden barrier jolted up and jolted down.

Who are all these people, who come to the hospital from nine to five, five days a week, just as if death and disease abide by normal business hours?

Inside, through the broad automatic sliding doors, it was like an airport. People were dashing in or out, or waiting anxiously, or talking on their phones, or drifting uncertainly; there were taxi numbers next to a big yellow payphone, a diagrammatical map on the wall as complicated as the London Underground, and arrowed signs for Outpatients and Maternity Suite and Hawthorne Unit. Some people even had little suitcases on wheels. There was a shop selling newspapers and sweets, and a bright canteen, where the staff were clattering crockery and wheeling out a stack of fresh trays.

On Sunday night, when I arrived, I asked the solitary man at the desk for directions to Marlowe Ward, and he said, enigmatically, "Follow the blue line, love." I discovered there were coloured lines on the floors of the corridors, bright colour-coded plastic strips to follow through the maze. The temptation was to follow the line as a child would, feet single file on the tightrope with no stepping off, follow-the-blue-line, follow-the-blue-line... where did the other lines go? The red line swerved suddenly into the frosted glass and potted plants of Outpatients; after a while the orange line dipped into Radiography. The grubby white line disappeared beneath a set of discreet double doors. Only blue and green were left; which would fall first? Blue... the blue line took a right turn, and deposited me in front of a list of ward names and arrows. The green line continued on, into the distance of the infinite corridor; I never found out where it went.

Back in my teenage years, when I liked to shock myself with horror and sci-fi, I read a short story that was about death. There was a party in an apartment; it was late and everyone was drinking and eating, dancing and laughing, but when, every now and then, someone decided to leave, pulling on their coat and kissing the air goodbye, they stepped out of the door to find there was nothing there, absolutely nothing. The whole world had been swallowed up by a black hole or something and all that was left was that one apartment. The departing guests were instantly annihilated by the black vacuum of space. As the story went on, it emerged that some of the people at the party knew that there was nothing outside but the void, but they still carried on laughing and dancing and chatting about nothing, because there was, after all, nothing they could do about the world being sucked into nothingness and they might as well enjoy this one last party. One of the characters, of course, couldn't cope with the truth when he found out, and after a hysterical scene he ran out the door, coatless, unable to wait any longer for his inevitable fate. The other guests shook their heads and carried on with the party.

The point of the story - a neat allegory, appealing to my teenage mind - was that we are all going to die, but we carry on living our lives, however petty and pointless, without thinking about death at all.

It seemed to me that the hospital was like a window into the void. If one of the partygoers in the warm, happy apartment was to pull open the curtains, he would be shocked at the absolute darkness outside, and quickly pull the curtain back across. This hospital was full of rooms where dying was actually happening. But the people around me were still trying not to think about the void at all, even when it was this close and the curtain was so flimsy; they were bustling about just as if they were in a cafe or a post office, like the partygoers with the curtains firmly closed.

I had rung work at nine o'clock, when I had claimed a space in the car park, and was sitting in my car, watching the busy people arriving. There were spindly trees bobbing in the breeze, each trapped in a little cage between the parking spaces. As I blurted my big news into the small phone I could hear Alison, the office

18

manager, breathing it all in and swelling with importance, ready to perform a mini-tragedy to the receptionists and clerks when she had put the phone down. "No, don't you worry," she said, "I'll get someone to cover your court; I'm sure we'll manage. Take as many days as you need; don't you worry about a thing." So there I was, released from work. I felt fraudulent; the grieving daughter. Alison probably loved her mother; probably went round for Sunday lunch and talked about Strictly. A normal relationship.

The parking ticket I had plucked from the machine was printed with the day and time, like a souvenir. I sat holding it, watching an elderly couple struggle with car doors and walking sticks. It must be hard being old: you must want to shake it off and move normally again. But I had to move, now; the nurses might be wondering where I was. Hasn't Amelia Nash's daughter arrived yet? We did tell her she could visit any time, didn't we?

Follow the blue line.

Only I'd forgotten about these shoes. I don't wear them often. I have my flat work shoes, and my trainers, and these sort-of-smart shoes, intended for all other occasions. Yesterday, caught by surprise, I was wearing my trainers, as usual for a weekend, but getting dressed for the hospital this morning I had agonised over what to wear and settled on black jeans and a plain top and these shoes. I'd forgotten that I have to wear a plaster on my heel or they rub. At first it's a little sting, a warning, and I try walking differently, sliding my weight forwards, and I think it'll be fine, I can put up with a bit of discomfort, it's just a shoe; but then real pain kicks in with every step and I know a patch of skin has ripped, and I find myself limping, gasping, step-ouch, step-ouch looking desperately for somewhere to buy plasters.

Following the blue line, I tried to ignore the rub, walking lightly, cursing my stupidity. The red line turned. The orange line turned. The blue line went on and on. Step-ouch, step-ouch.

I could have gone back to the hospital shop, but I was so close to the ward and it was already past nine o'clock. Were the nurses wondering where I was? Has she slept in, has she stopped for breakfast, doesn't she know her mother's dying? I limped along the blue line. Here, in a hospital full of broken legs and cancer, I was limping because of a rubbing shoe.

Marlowe Ward. There was a woman at the door before me and she turned to smile at me. I smiled back. She wore a suit, sleek hair and a laminated ID card round her neck on a chain. We took turns with the antibacterial gel dispenser on the wall, a public spirited ritual before entering the ward, like genuflecting or removing the shoes. As we stood there, wringing our hands, the door buzzed and a huge trolley came through; we stood aside as the trolley, a sturdy medicine box on wheels, knocked open both doors and cornered awkwardly into the corridor, the porter behind it nodding to us both and sliding away. We caught the uneven doors before they closed and went through into the ward.

Should I have announced myself to the intercom? No-one seemed to mind me; there was bustle and purpose. and several nurses made eye contact with me and just smiled, without questions. I limped down the corridor, trying not to limp, trying small, slow steps, trying big ones, trying to walk on one side of my foot. Nash, said the black writing on the whiteboard. My name, too. There were black smudges where other names had been hastily wiped and new scribbles where new names had been added. There was a commotion in one of the rooms, but my mother's room was calm and orderly. I limped across to her and sat down. My chair, the same chair, was in the same place, waiting for me.

She had moved - or rather, been moved - and she was wearing a different nightie, this one blue and white. When I looked at the fabric, scumbled from so many washings, I saw that it was a frenetic pattern of blue birds and dolphins on an off-white background. She had been propped into a different position, and today her eyelids looked heavier, and the eyes inside were small and greasy. I guessed the nurses used eyedrops for patients who couldn't blink for themselves. Her breathing was still fast and mechanical, a chain of snores rising to a loud grunt, then a few quiet breaths, and then snores rising again. I sat and looked at her.

"Hello, Mum," I said. My voice was very quiet.

"Hello, Mum," I said, louder. "It's me, again."

20

When I was a child, my favourite toys were a family of dolls ' house figures. Their house became shabby over the years, the wallpaper torn and crayoned, and the legs came unstuck from tables and beds, but I kept the figures even after the house was given away. I played with them in a drawer, on my pillow or in a pocket. They were soft little people made from wool and felt, with beautiful tiny faces: their eyes and mouths were just dots on pale pink cloth and they looked sensitive and vulnerable. There was a boy called John, who wore orange felt dungarees and a worried face, and a girl called Ellie, whose hair was an oversized clump of brown wool, gathered behind her neck with a taut ribbon and then flaring out like a fat tassel. I used to swirl her hair round and round in my fingers when I held her in my pocket. There were parents, too, but they were just minor characters to me. The mother had a slightly crooked face and a long, funnel shaped felt dress, too stiff for her to sit down, so she always stood. The father had yellow wool hair and a curious cloth neckerchief, and I always had the feeling that he was foreign, German or Swiss or something. He seemed very kind and gentle. He sat well: his legs were long and grasshopperish and it was satisfying to bend them fully so he could sit on the floor with his knees against his chest. He sometimes told the children bedtime stories.

When we moved into the house in Lucas Street, the little doll family moved too, and enjoyed exploring my new room, scaling the skirting boards and making their beds in a drawer, amongst my clothes. They were happy with their new home. By then, though, they were ageing: John's dungarees had a loose thread, and then one day his leg wouldn't bend properly when he sat, but insisted on drooping down straight. I realised then that beneath their sturdy felt clothes their bodies were made of wire wrapped round and round in yards of wool, like mummies wrapped in bandages. The wire of John's leg had snapped at the hip, although the leg was still firmly held by the coil of pink wool and the stiff orange dungarees, so it wouldn't detach from him. John could no longer sit, but I knew he loved to climb, and I would bend his elbows and knees into athletic angles so he could scramble up the pillow or reach for the bedhead.

Ellie's hand started to unravel, the pink wool developing a small loop and then a spiral; the glue must have relaxed, and every day I had to carefully re-wrap her arm before she sat down to breakfast. I could feel her legs becoming brittle and unpredictable, and for fear that the wire would snap, she took to her bed. Ellie became an invalid, swaddled in a sock sleeping bag, while her father squatted beside her and told her happy stories.

I could pick Ellie up in her sock and hold her safe in my hand, twirling her hair, and I liked it that she was sick, because she needed my protection. I liked to feel that I was strong, strong enough to be a protector, not vulnerable and in need of protection myself.

We moved to the house in Lucas Street because in the end Dad let the building society take our house. Mum said we would "fight them all the bloody way". We made plans. We would change the locks and draw the curtains and never answer the door. We would pour concrete into the locks and use a rope from an upstairs window when we needed to get in or out. We would nail shut all the windows and drag the fridge behind the door; we would make little explosives from fireworks and put them in front of the door; we would string tripwires in the garden, drop flour bombs from the windows and dig a hole under the mat. But then Mum went to see the house at Lucas Street and one day she met me from school with a borrowed key. "It's so modern," she insisted, "the kitchen's practically new, with granite worktops, and the loo's got one of those double flush buttons..." and she went on to explain that renting was actually much better than owning a house. We were free from responsibility, she said. It became our little song: 'What do we do if the roof leaks?' 'Call the landlord!' 'What do we do if the shower breaks?' 'Call the landlord!' 'What do we do if the boiler won't light?' 'Call the landlord! 'Everything she had said before, about our home being our home forever, about protecting it to her final breath, was swept away like dust. And then we were packed and excited and suddenly ready to move.

My mother advanced through life like a motorway, shaping the landscape around her as she went.

A nurse appeared. She smiled and said that Dr Amin wanted to speak to me and would be along soon, and then she checked over my mother, squeezing her wrist, tugging her bedding, observing the monitor. She ripped a new pink foam lollipop from its packaging and deftly ran it round the inside of my mother's inert mouth. I sat watching, pressed back into my big chair. Perhaps the nurse thought I should be more tender with my mother, holding her hand, or stroking her hair... is that what daughters do? But it had been so many years since I had touched her. I sat still, in the big chair.

After the nurse had gone, some visitors came for the bed behind me. They dragged chairs from across the room and talked boisterously about traffic and weather. I didn't hear the person in the bed say anything. After a while they left, drifting out of the door, pulling on jackets and talking with mild anxiety about the system in the car park, wondering to each other whether they should have paid and displayed or whether there was one of those machines at the exit.

After they had gone the ward was quiet, and I sat deeply in my big chair, waiting for Dr Amin. Neither my mother nor I moved, or said anything. A different nurse, in a different uniform, came to the next bed and called "Celia, would you like a cup of tea? Celia?" I hadn't looked properly at Celia but I now saw that she was swaddled in sheets and in an uncertain state of consciousness. It seemed she was refusing tea. The nurse went away.

I realised that I was starting to feel comfortable here: my chair was becoming familiar, and the smell of the ward was no longer strange. I was adapting. I had my chair and I was doing my duty, sitting at my mother's bedside, waiting for Dr Amin. I would have liked a cup of tea myself.

I had given up trying to talk to my mother. The reason wasn't diffidence or fear or grief. I couldn't say anything because every time I thought of something to say, and imagined saying it, my imagination blurted out the reply my mother would have given if she had been conscious.

"I love you, Mum."

"Do you really? How nice for you."

"I just want you to know I'm here."

"Is that supposed to make me feel better?"

"I'm staying right here, Mum…"

"Why? You don't care about me. You tried to fuck my life up. Why are you here now?"

The conversation in my head was becoming fraught, so I stopped it, and sat in silence.

Of course, this wasn't the first time I had visited her in hospital.

A different ward, a different hospital, a different time. She was young and strong then; she was passionate and explosive, the opposite of unconscious. They called it Acorn Ward, the psychiatric ward, and the nurse looked at me and then said to Mark, in a discreet tone," How old is she? We don't like children to visit this ward…" A ward too distressing for children. Before then, I had always pictured hospital wards as rooms full of beds, but in a psychiatric ward the patients aren't sick and don't need to lie down, so were there no beds? What was a hospital ward without beds? It sounded like a riddle. "She's fifteen," Mark said. "I think she's old enough." I held Mark's arm, and he squeezed mine, as if we were comrades, plunging into the ward together.

That was twenty years ago. I loved her then: fiercely, helplessly.

"I'm sorry about everything, Mum."

"Too late for that now, isn't it?"

Everything in my head was moving a bit too quickly and I suddenly had to get up out of my chair and move. I took strides to the door, purposefully, ostensibly to look for Dr Amin. Once there, though, all I could do was wait, looking this way and that along the corridor, like an impatient traveller on a station platform who doesn't know which direction the train will come from.

Two nurses went by quickly, and a cleaner came from the opposite direction with a grotesquely long handled dustpan and brush. The nurses appeared to be colour-coded, in different uniforms: some wore brown dresses, pinched in the middle with fat elastic belts; others were in blue, some in trousers and some in skirts. I wear a black gown at work. It's made of matt black cotton, like darkness itself, a wearable shadow; the gown is huge and

24

hangs in folds around me, but doesn't fasten at the front, so I have to wear black clothes underneath. Sometimes the gown flies out behind me, like a cape or a vampiric cloak, if I have to rush with a message: the trailing gown, lifted by my haste, signals to people to step aside deferentially to let me through. It's almost more of a costume than a uniform: an antiquated outfit, as formal and eccentric as a judge's wig.

In the gown I am an usher, not myself. The magic of uniforms is that they turn people into functions - policeman, nurse, fireman. The security guard on the front desk at court wears a black pullover and a tie and a bored expression; he waves a chunky plastic paddle, a metal detector, and it lets out electronic squeaks and squeals. He is a human barrier. The custody officers are in sand-coloured uniforms, jangling keys; they are serious, mostly overweight men and their job is to bring the prisoners into the courtroom and take them away again through the blank locked door behind the dock. Sometimes they are called to take a defendant into custody, if they're sentenced to prison. The defendant sits in the dock, waiting with the rest of us for the magistrates to come back in and announce their decision. Meanwhile, the magistrates, who retired to their back room to discuss him, have decided to impose a prison sentence, and they have telephoned the custody officers to warn them to be ready. Behind the blank door there is a muffled, sinister sound of keys and shuffling, and then a pause, and everyone in the courtroom knows that the man in the dock is about to be taken away. Usually he knows, too - they're usually regulars and they know what the sounds mean, but they always stay in the dock, shoulders sinking, sighing. They never try to run. The magistrates come back in and everyone has to stand, and then everyone sits and the magistrate in the middle begins to announce the decision and even as he is speaking the custody officers come rattling and slamming through the door, and the magistrate seems almost irrelevant as he stumbles through the script he has to read: "…this offence is so serious that only a custodial sentence will merit the…"

The magistrates don't wear uniforms, which is incongruous, because it means they look like real people. When announcing the sentence, they squirm under the responsibility. They should be allowed to wear uniforms, like judges, who hide their personal selves beneath wigs and gowns.

Dr Amin came. He was wearing a casually unbuttoned white coat and a laminated ID on a cord swinging from his neck. He tried to find a private room for us to speak in, and I followed him up and down the corridor, starting and stopping and smiling apologetically when he expressed frustration. My heel stung me with every step and I limped and winced. Eventually we sat at the nurses 'station, behind the high counter, on two high stools, like bar stools, or stools in those cafes where you grab a quick sandwich. He started explaining strokes to me, and then he wanted to show me my mother's CT scan, so we set off again in search of a computer. They were all in use until Dr Amin snapped at someone, and then he poked the keyboard for a long time until the screen showed a glowing cross-section of a brain.

"Hah!" he triumphed." This is it." There was an enormous egg-shaped black patch in the glowing brain. He clicked through a series of slices of brain, the black patch expanding and contracting along with the skull, and he talked about brain function and viability and the obvious impossibility of operating. Then he became kind and regretful and said they would move my mother to a single room as soon as one became available.

I remember, many years ago, my mother was fascinated by a news story about a man who had amnesia. A boating accident had knocked him unconscious, and when he woke up he could remember nothing about his life or who he had been. He couldn't recognise relatives or recall names, couldn't remember places or events, and was a stranger to his own house. It sounded terrifying to me, but my mother was taken with the idea of rebirth." You could start again as a completely different person, anyone you wanted to be." It was her greatest wish to be born afresh every minute, unimpeded by past or future. "Here and now," she used to say, "living in the here and now." When she was drunk she often spoke of regrets and guilt, and the past as a weight she was condemned to drag behind her, a life sentence in retrospect. "I'm such a fuck up," she spat, when she was drunk, "such a fucking fuck up." When sober, though, it was the present that bothered her: "What is that fucking smell?"

For the rented house in Lucas Street had a smell. We didn't speak of it at first. Mum laughed at the fact that the crisp new doors of the kitchen cupboards concealed formica interiors that were yellow from age and fatigue, and speckled with brown blotches like old skin. The squeaky new carpets had been hastily fitted: they were bunched at the edges and buckled in the doorways so that the doors scraped or stuck. "Cheap carpets," my mum said, but it didn't matter, because we didn't own them. We were unfettered, just passing through, no obligation, no responsibility. We laughed at the wobbly curtain pole.

But as the months passed it became, by necessity, our home. Habit sent my feet the right way out of school, past the new houses and the old shops, slowing my pace to avoid the kids I didn't like or quickening to catch up with those I did. In my class we were choosing which high school to go to the following year. This band of children, who I had known, it seemed, all my life, were to split in two: half I would continue on with to a new school, half I would never see again. We were like a nomadic tribe driven to the edge of its barren hunting grounds, each individual choosing whether to follow one leader into the unknown hills to the north, or the other leader into the unknown plains to the south. "You may as well toss a coin," my mother said. School didn't interest her: she said the choice was up to me. I had the brochures of both schools, and I examined the photos of shiny children and the bland, smooth text like someone searching for a prophecy in the entrails of a goat.

Meanwhile, the smell in the house crept up on us, occasionally glimpsed but not quite apprehended, easily ignored at first as we got on with our lives, until one day one of us commented on it - and then it was definitely there, peripheral but persistent. Mum bought some stuff for the drains in a bright orange bottle, and glugged it down the sinks, impatiently waiting the recommended five minutes before chasing it with steaming water from the kettle. She hunted down a damp patch in the cupboard under the sink and scrubbed it violently. She hoovered all the carpets and bleached the toilet. The smell ignored her. It was hard to say exactly where it was coming from: walking from one room to another, the smell would drift as if it had come from the room I had just left; but when I walked back it had gone. We sniffed deeply, frowning, poking in corners. It was impossible to describe, too: not quite rotten, not quite chemical, not quite mould, it was a very particular smell, yet at times it was sudden and rich and at other times faint and diffuse and lingering. We decided it was downstairs, only to doubt ourselves, calling one another upstairs as if we could catch our quarry in a pincer movement. We stalked it into the bedrooms only for it to scatter.

The hall carpet came unpinned behind the front door, and Mum called the landlord, who sent a man with a staple gun to subdue it. The blind in the bathroom collapsed shockingly on my head; I wasn't hurt, but Mum shouted into the phone and an elderly odd job man came round to re-attach it. He stayed for hours, standing in the bathroom sipping tea and chatting to Mum, and I was too embarrassed to ask them to leave so I could use the toilet. The kitchen tap dribbled, the boiler made a funny noise and there were interesting cracks in the ceiling above my bed.

The smell went beyond all these irritations, though. It was mild yet sinister, a hint of hidden darkness. My mother started to talk about rats beneath the floorboards, rising damp in the walls, or wet rot under the bath. It seemed to me that the house was wearing a mask: beneath the new carpets and cupboard doors was something grotesque and filthy. In the night I imagined maggots and blood, fungus and decay, and I listened for the sound of scratching, gnawing or skittering under the floors. After a while I didn't want to touch the floor with my bare feet, or even socks, so I carefully changed from shoes to slippers at the door when I arrived home, and stepped out of the bath onto the cork mat as if it were a little raft.

I began to recoil from the walls, too, and eventually I dragged my bed into the middle of my room, like an island. My bedroom walls were papered with wood-chip - "What have they covered up with that, eh?" Mum said - and painted white; they looked cold, and I imagined them to be damp to the touch. I didn't want to touch them to find out. When my bedside light was on, the little pieces of wood-chip cast tiny dark shadows like a thousand ants on the wall. When I turned out the light the streetlamp lit my curtain and I pretended it was the moon, peacefully guiding my safe, floating bed.

Mum bought gallons of bleach, and when I walked in from school that day the shock of it almost made me sick. It was a thick, choking smell that soaked though the whole house; I refused to eat and cried, and Mum and I shouted at each other and ended up agreeing it was all my father's fault. That night I put my head out of the window to escape the bleach, and in the cold, clear air the street glowed yellow beneath the lamps like a fairground. I wondered if the bleach had poisoned me.

The next day was a Saturday. We made up and she took me out for the day to escape the bleach. We went into town and looked at clothes and she bought me a Polly Pocket doll set. We had lunch in a department store, sliding our tray in the queue between clumps of little old ladies; I had cheese and pickle sandwiches encased in a plastic prism and a round red jelly topped with a hemisphere of cream.

We stayed out until it started to get dark, and Mum said we would have tea out too. The lit shops were exciting beneath the darkening sky, and high overhead starlings were swirling noisily, seeking out rooftops that weren't defended by spikes or netting. At one point they descended around a man who had been feeding pigeons, and as they clustered around him I saw their plumage change from black to purple and green. We went into a fancy cafe bar called Barracuda, and ordered burgers and chips. The burgers were so multi-layered that they were skewered with sticks to hold them together, and the chips were fat and crisp, with the skin left on. We were happy, giggling about how difficult it was to manhandle the burgers; Mum said they should come with instructions. It was dark outside and the shops had closed and it felt like the world of grown-ups.

"Perhaps we just shouldn't go back," said Mum, wiping her hands on a napkin. "Sod it. Sod that stinking house." She looked happy, fired up and strong. "We could just walk out of here and start a new life. Change our names. What do you think?"

29

I suppose that's the difference between being a parent and being a child. Freedom and choice for the one means, for the other, being attached to a rollercoaster. I was a passenger in someone else's life. We all are, as children. Perhaps some of us are as adults too. Perhaps that was why my father left.

"I'd do it," she went on, "if I had the money. It's always about the bloody money. If I had the money I'd just move around, Paris this week, Marrakesh next; live the high life in a big city and then retreat to the wilds of nowhere, pump water from a well and grow my own veg. Try everything, meet everyone. Be everyone. I don't want to be a little old lady, looking back over my life and thinking 'what did I do?' I want to sit in my chair in my old age remembering all my adventures and laughing."

She paid the bill and we walked to the bus stop. The night air was chilly, and there were people going out to pubs and clubs. My mother seemed enlivened, and didn't want to go home, not ever. She lit a cigarette. "We could just buy two train tickets, to anywhere..."

I was relieved when we got on the bus and went home.

Over the next few days the bleach smell faded; but the other smell was still there, waiting.

"It's like it's bloody mocking us!" my mum shouted, as she slammed the kitchen cupboards, but to me the smell was inanimate: it wasn't a creature with a will, but an ineluctable force, without purpose or emotion, like steadily rising flood water. My mother ripped the carpets up from their fierce upturned nails and peeled them back, but the dusty floorboards were dry. She knocked out the u-bend under the sink, cracking the plastic and releasing some promising gunk, but even after she had lied to a plumber to get the pipe renewed the smell was still there. She asked the plumber's opinion on the smell but he just pulled a face and shrugged. She sprayed water on the walls, scrubbed them and stained them. She was convinced there was something baked into the building, some ingredient in the brick or the plaster or the wood.

Then one night she woke me up.

30

"The cavity," she hissed. "I've got it. I bet there's a cavity in the wall, a gap between the outer skin and the inside. I bet something's growing there." She had a hammer.

I was balancing on one foot next to the washbasins, trying to lean against the yellow wall without setting off the hand dryer or catching sinister germs. The hospital toilets smelled of heavy duty lemon disinfectant, and the row of cubicles behind me kept flushing and discharging women into the narrow space beside me, where they struggled to operate the baffling modern taps and effusive pink soap dispensers. I was balancing on one foot and obstructing the hand dryer because I was trying to stick a plaster onto the right place on my heel, only the sticky parts kept curling up and trying to stick to each other.

No longer limping, I sought out food. There was a small kiosk near the sliding entrance doors, and I wondered if a quick snack was more appropriate than a meal in the canteen: how could I eat at a time like this? A proper lunch seemed somehow disrespectful to the purpose of my visit. The kiosk was staffed by a guard of white-haired lady volunteers, attending solicitously to a big shiny tea urn and cross-examining each other about the location of the clean cups. There's a similar kiosk at the magistrates court where I work, except they dispense tea into corrugated cardboard cups, which the defendants fill with cigarette ends on the steps outside. The defendants aren't supposed to go outside and smoke; when they arrive we tell them that they have answered their bail and they are now in the custody of the court and forbidden from leaving: the corridor is effectively a prison, as are the benches and the kiosk itself. The regulars go out onto the steps to smoke anyway; they seem to see the red brick flight of stairs as part of the court building, part of the great penal edifice. The ones who aren't regulars sit on the benches inside, unsettled when they discover that all the cases are listed for ten o 'clock, not just theirs, and they might be waiting all morning; wavering between outrage and humiliation, they hop up from the benches as we pass and follow us, trying politely to attract our attention, and we have to inform them that the cases are not called in the order on the list but in the order that suits the clerk. They are not customers but raw materials, here to be processed.

I was hungry. Beside the tea urn was a basket of little plastic-wrapped biscuits - digestive, ginger, bourbon or garibaldi - and to my empty stomach they seemed simultaneously meagre and rich. I walked across to the canteen. Was it wrong to eat properly? Would my mother die while I was stuffing down a jacket potato? I suddenly felt tired. There was no-one watching me, after all, no chorus or jury to disapprove. I joined the queue with my tray.

The canteen was teeming: hospital staff, busy and loud, clattered and chatted around the slow-moving, slightly bewildered civilians. I found a small table and stirred a paper tube of sugar into my tea. My baked potato and beans had been served on top of a wet yellow salad, and the beans were dark and congealed in places. At the next table sat a bearded man opposite a smartly dressed woman; he mumbled continually and inaudibly while she occasionally responded loudly and distinctly, so that she sounded like one side of a telephone conversation. "So were you drinking every day by that time?" she asked, forcefully. "Was that when you realised you had depression?" At the table on my other side sat a group of administrative staff members in suits, big ID cards hanging from them, showing each other important paperwork and sipping coffee. Eventually they rose, adjusting their clothes, rubbing their eyes and tucking away their phones, and one man collected all their cups and jangled over to the kitchen hatch helpfully. Two middle-aged women took their table, talking about the existence or otherwise of mayonnaise.

I ate. The potato was a bit hard in the middle.

The two middle-aged women were talking about someone called Janet. "Ooh yes, I kept in touch with her," one was saying, as she tried to extract herself from her lemon-coloured jacket by jerking her shoulders repeatedly and tugging at her cuffs behind her back. "Ooh, sorry, love" - she had caught a neighbouring diner with her jacket - "yes, I met her husband, too, years ago now."

The other woman was already chewing and her jaw didn't pause." Mmm?"

"Yes, well, you remember she was seeing that Eddie chap, but they split up, and she met a postman, Richard, and they got married and had kids and moved out to Easterly... she had a boy, can't remember his name, and a girl a few years later, and she worked in a newsagents for a time but she had trouble with her hip. She's retired now. And the boy works in computers, he moved away, and the girl's at university, studying, oh, media or something."

A whole life in one short story. They moved on to talk about hips and backs and sciatica, having reduced Janet to a light and dull life story.

We all feel that our lives are rich and complicated, but to everyone else we're just "that woman at number twenty-three" or "the bald bloke that works in the cafe". Sometimes I bump into an acquaintance who says: "I haven't seen you in weeks! What have you been up to?" and I can think of nothing, absolutely nothing, to say. I am embarrassed by my mundanity, my world of microwave dinners and walks to work and evenings watching TV, and if, later, I think of something interesting I have done - been to the cinema or bought new shoes - I want to run after her to tell her yes, I've thought of something, I have done something in the last eight weeks.

My mother, of course, was never boring. At the house in Lucas Street she took a hammer to the wall in the middle of the night. I expected the wall to shatter, collapsing into rubble, but at first it just dented, revealing a half moon of greyish white plaster beneath the clean yellow paint. My mother hit it again, swinging the hammer in a glorious wide arc, and there was another, bigger dent, and more dents getting broader and deeper as she pounded, until plaster and paint began to break away and fall to the floor in clumps and dust.

It was frightening, seeing a hole open up in the wall. Our sitting room was a normal, tidy room, the furniture sitting innocently still and undisturbed, only now there was a gash in the wall, grey and growing, spraying chalky white dust all over the new carpet, and it seemed sudden and irreversible, like an avalanche or a car crash. My mother was panting and her neck was red. "This bloody house won't get the better of me!" she shouted, and started swinging the hammer again, mechanical and vigorous, angry and eager. I wanted her to stop but she didn't even hear me.

My watch showed the time as three o'clock, but it looked wrong, the wrong three o'clock: not the afternoon that I was familiar with but a macabre, alternative three o'clock, the night-time three o'clock, out of shift with the normal world, a time outside of time when terrible things could happen. The electric lights were coarse and unnatural. I had the feeling that everyone else in the world was asleep, and my mother would have time to destroy everything before the world woke up, too late to stop her.

She had exposed brick, and chips and shards were splintering under the slam of the hammer. The noise was tremendous but the rest of the world still slept out there in the comfortable, gentle darkness. The plaster dust made me cough and cry. My mother was infuriated by the immutable brick and she moved on to another wall, the internal one between the sitting room and the kitchen, and she was elated when the hammer head punched right through, crunching wood and plaster and suddenly smashing kitchen tiles. She kept going, lacerating the wall with her hammer and ripping at it with her bare red hands, distorting space itself so that I could see straight through from the sitting room to the oven.

The decor of the house, the fresh carpets and new curtains and genial walls, were all irrelevant now, as the guts slid out of the mangled walls. Ragged lumps of plaster were crushed underfoot. I looked at my watch again and it was only five past three; it was then that I understood for the first time just how long the night is, all those hours between midnight, which felt so late, and six, which felt so early; those long hours of metamorphosis while everyone slept. My mother had time enough to smash every particle of the house.

"Let's go to bed," I begged, "I'm tired." I wasn't really tired at all. I had never been so far from feeling sleepy. My mother was laughing. She was so far gone into the deep, euphoric tunnel she was digging that nothing could reach her. She was attacking the ceiling.

"No, that's dangerous," I said, but my voice sounded strange and muted. She had stepped up on to the settee, striking the pose of a mountaineer with one foot raised boldly on the back of the seat. She swung her hammer and the ceiling smashed like a meringue, whitening her hair and eyebrows and shoulders. She coughed and giggled and swung again and again, opening up a view of floorboards, dust and cobwebs, like a mini-attic between the storeys of the house.

"Let's go to bed," I whispered, but it was too late. The house was lost, wrecked, ruined, and maybe on the brink of cascading down onto our heads; I ran into the kitchen and stood with my bare feet on the cold linoleum, shivering and watching the shower of plaster and dust through the hole in the wall. My mother was swearing breathlessly, beating the intractable floorboards above her. She suddenly stopped, and paused, her powdered face upturned to the ceiling and her eyes and lips moving as she thought. For a moment I wondered if she had found something horrible, but I couldn't will myself to move forward to see its face. But there was nothing; it was an idea that had stilled her.

"The attic," she said at last. "That bloody attic. I bet there's a body up there."

She skipped down from the settee and went upstairs with light steps, and when I followed I found her on the landing, wheeling my desk chair out of my bedroom. "Hold this, will you?" she said, without looking at me. I gripped the back of the swivel chair while she scrambled on to it, her forcefulness almost wrenching it out of my hands. The loft had a recessed square door, like a lid, which she pushed up with both hands and threw aside. The chair wobbled and tried to twist and I nearly fell over. To climb up into the hole, she had to put one foot on the flimsy back of the chair and then heave up, balancing on that one foot while the chair wriggled in my hands. She bumped herself up into the dark attic and disappeared.

There was scraping and creaking and thumping and muttering. The chair in my hands now felt light and compliant. I didn't let go. I was looking upwards so intently that my throat hurt. Eventually her leg came pointing down, and then the rest of her, slithering, sending the chair skittering - "Watch it!" - but she somehow found the truculent seat with both feet, and stepped down to the floor. "Fuck," she said, looking at her knee, which was bleeding through her trousers.

"Too fucking dark," she went on, "but I don't reckon there's anything up there. Where the bloody hell is it?"

Then she started to cry.

"You must have been terrified when she set fire to the house," Mark said.

This was four years later. Mark and I were sitting on a bench outside the psychiatric ward, Acorn Ward, in a small garden enclosed between corridors, opposite a woman in a dressing gown who was sitting on the other bench, smoking. There was a square of fractured paving stones between us and a border of small-leaved ornamental bushes, which shivered in the breeze.

Mark was the only other person in the whole world who came to know the truth about how the fire started, and by the time I spoke about it to him I had nearly forgotten that the story we had been telling everyone else, for years, was a lie. The tale Mum and I told - waking up to smoke, clutching bannisters in the dark, escaping through the kitchen from the hot, crackling sitting room - had been told so many times, repeated, clarified and enhanced, that it had become as plump and familiar as memory; while the truth had never been spoken, and without nourishment it had shrivelled up and faded away.

So when Mark asked me, I had to scratch up those dry, brittle bits of memory and make of them a new story, a story based in truth, but with so little truth available I did perhaps add a little in the restoration. In the little hospital garden, the bushes bobbed in the breeze, clenching in sudden spasms when the wind caught them, and I shivered too, and Mark put his arm round me and said I was a brave girl.

The funny thing was how difficult it was to start the fire. Mum got a cigarette glowing and dropped it on the settee, but it just rolled a little and dimmed unhappily. She had to try again and again, pressing it down and re-lighting it, until we were both giggling wildly at the ridiculousness of what we were doing. She

36

was calm now, and purposeful, and - strangely - whispering. There had been some wailing and shouting, and the hammer had been thrown across the room, but the atmosphere had now changed, and we were whispering. We had a plan: a plan to burn the ruined house to the ground before the rest of the world woke up.

She had to use the lighter to help it along. The settee cover was a rich, velvety red, and it suddenly shrank away, retreating in all directions from the flame that had caught the fabric underneath, which was white and cottony and turning black. We stepped back, watching anxiously. There was smoke and then the whole settee began to smoulder, and then there was a terrific smell, a sharp, caustic, burning smell. "Let's be sure," Mum said, and she took hold of the curtain and dipped it into the fire, and we watched, coughing, as the fabric scorched and withered.

There was a smoke alarm on the landing upstairs, but its beeping was tinny and remote. "Just another minute," Mum whispered. There was a lot of smoke. The smoke was a heavy, dark grey, like a storm cloud, or a felt prison blanket, or the thick matted dust inside a vacuum cleaner; it drifted and twisted and grew magnificent, like a thunderstorm rising in the sky. We were choking and we had to leave, staggering to the back door through the intoxicating smell. Outside, in the back yard, everything was cold, dark and hard, and the world really was, incredibly, still asleep. Mum had her phone in her hand but she just stood waiting, watching the house. She had shut the back door and the house looked shockingly dark and still, quiet except for the muffled smoke alarm, twittering away to itself deep inside.

"How did you feel?" Mark asked, gently.

"Just cold," I said. It sounded very profound, and that was when he put his arm around me.

I was doing it again. Filling in her side of the conversation.

"Hi, Mum, I'm back."

"I don't know why you bothered."

"I went for lunch. I had a baked potato."

"Do you think I care?" She had an answer for everything.

She had been moved again. The nurses were efficient, shifting her around two or three times a day, wetting her mouth, doing the things they had to do to keep her ticking over. I sat and listened to her breathing, fast and coarse, and after a while it made me feel breathless and I had to focus on something else. Every now and then her breathing would hesitate, as people pause when they're asleep, and then she would take a big, rattling breath, and snort. Nothing else about her moved, so she was like a breathing machine, chest rising and falling, air rushing backwards and then forwards. I tried to think about something else.

"I was just thinking," I said, "I was just thinking about the fire. In Lucas Street."

I would never have said that to her when she was conscious. Not because it wasn't spoken of, but because when she did speak of it she twisted it more and more to her own advantage. "We were so unlucky with that fire," she would say. "We lost everything in that fire." Or: "That fire - that was where everything really went wrong. That was what crushed me." I hated it when she wallowed in self pity; it was like drowning, and she spoke slowly and reflectively as she held us both under. "We had nothing left but the clothes we stood up in; we had to start all over again." She would talk like this to her friends, to my friends, to strangers, to me. "We lost everything that night. Even those little dolls you played with…"

When she said that, I protected myself from the awful truth by mentally separating" those little dolls you played with" from the dolls I knew, so that she was talking about something completely different, something that didn't matter at all; and then I could believe that my doll family still existed, I still had them, I just hadn't got them out in a long time. Ellie and John and their parents; I could imagine I had rescued them from the fire and kept them safe. After all, in my memory they were as real as if they were in my hands, and I could imagine that they were right there, in a drawer, or in a bag, and I could get them out right now if I wanted to. I couldn't ever let myself think about what had really happened to my little doll family.

So it was nice to bring up the subject of the fire now, when she could say nothing. She was silenced.

"That fire," I said, out loud. "It was... I suppose it was... a fresh start. You got your fresh start."

She said nothing.

I sat there for a long time without speaking, and eventually got up to stretch my legs. Outside Marlowe Ward the long corridor had been hung with art from a local amateurs 'club, and I worked my way dutifully along the row of pictures, looking carefully at each one. Other people walked by, quickly or slowly, without stopping or looking. The images were startlingly unconnected: a pencil drawing of a dog, artfully smudged; a tiny flat watercolour of a sunset; a giant swirling abstract in thick, crusty acrylic. At least they hadn't papered the walls like a GP's waiting room, with grim posters about flu jabs, meningitis and eating five a day. I looked at each picture and tried to think which I liked best, but they were all too different to compare. Further down the corridor were trolley beds, lined up against the wall like taxis.

When I went back to the room my mother was still alive. I sat back down in my chair and tried to think of something non-contentious to say. Normal visiting hours had begun, and people had come in from outside, carrying magazines and flowers, asking questions and pulling chairs up to beds. There were unexpected bursts of laughter from the room next door and the rumble of a woman wheeling a suitcase down the corridor outside. I sat very still and felt like a rock in one of those time-lapse nature films, where the tides rush in and out and the trees quiver and the clouds spin across the sky.

A woman came bustling into the room, scraping a chair up to the old lady in the next bed.

"Hello, Mum," she shouted. "How are we feeling today?"

Her mother was deep in the pillow, white against white, and she made a pale noise that could have meant anything.

"You're looking better." The woman was about forty, dressed in grey with an orange scarf, elegantly rumpled hair and a chunky silver bracelet draped over her slim wrist. She opened a hessian bag and pulled out a wad of shiny magazines. "I brought you something to read. Have they given you fresh water?"

All the beds had bedside cabinets, topped with lidded plastic jugs of water. The woman didn't sit down but instead started to investigate the jug. "You must ask for a drink when you need one," she instructed. "Don't suffer in silence, Mum, I've told you before." She leaned over the bed and started re-arranging the pillows and her mother.

There was a proper daughter: coming in and taking over. I don't know how parent-child relationships switch like that, the child becoming the parent, as if the two of them are on a seesaw. A lot of the women I know at work have changed position in that way: the office staff are all women in their thirties or forties, sharing complicated part-time hours and managing young children and elderly parents, taking charge of everyone. All the talk is about school uniforms and lunchboxes, statins and dementia.

The ushers are all older: semi-retired men and women who used to be something else. None of them are as young as me. It's not a young person's job. No-one tells their school careers advisor that they want to be an usher when they grow up. The other ushers, being older, have a tired respectability about them, an unshockable authority; because I'm younger, under forty, I'm the one who's sent on errands, nipping down to the cells with the paperwork or popping out onto the front steps to see if the missing defendant has gone for a smoke. Alison often puts me on the busy courts, the long mixed lists of adjournments and committals and whatever-comes-through-the-door, the lists that set the computers stuttering and the clerks scowling.

The proper daughter finished adjusting her mother and perched on her seat, leaning forward to broadcast a story about her washing machine breaking down. Then she stood up again and poured some water into a beaker, which she held insistently to her mother's wobbling lips. "You must remember to have a drink, Mum," she shouted. "You mustn't get dehydrated." Then she sat down again and said that Charlotte had been made class captain and William had played in a football match. Then she stood up again, re-examined the pillows, and left.

It was late when I went again in search of food. The canteen was dark behind a cage of shutters, the kiosk ladies had gone and even the shop was being swept. I found a snack machine dispensing chocolate and crisps, and a drinks machine that dropped first a plastic cup, then some brown powder, and then some scalding water, in exchange for three pound coins. The corridors were quiet and a porter was whistling, and as I walked slowly, balancing my small hot cup overfilled with coffee, past the arrow for the maternity ward, I thought idly that all those new people being born didn't make up for the stupid tragedy of dying.

My mother hadn't changed. Her breathing was still loud and constant, and nothing suggested decline, a slide towards death. Would there be a gradual slide? Or would she suddenly stop? A sudden stop would be terrifying. Would I shout for a nurse? It was getting late and my thoughts were stumbling. It seemed likely that she would die during the long bleak hours of the night - the proper time for death - but I couldn't, surely, stay here all night, through the longest hours, in this chair, dried out and exhausted, only for dawn to come at last and nothing to have happened. It would be worse, then, if I went home to sleep and she died in broad daylight, with me at home in bed - how would that look? They were difficult, these questions of etiquette... and why was I so cold and unfeeling? Surely I would want to be at her side?

I sat and drifted. I had noticed that all the furniture in the room was on wheels: everything was mobile and transient, like the scenery in a theatre. People could be shifted in and out, the machines changed and the equipment reconfigured. The whole room could be cleared out and expunged, completely sterilised. They could roll in more beds, roll out one patient and roll in another, rubbing names off the whiteboard and scribbling up new ones. It was not a room for resting in, but a busy junction.

How long could a person live without food or water? I remembered reading of people dying in the desert in less than a day, but what if they weren't moving, or speaking, or functioning at all except for breathing, like a machine on standby, operating on backup battery power only... Could she live for more than twenty-four hours, more than forty-eight? I couldn't think of a way to ask a nurse without sounding heartless and impatient. I considered googling how long, but that would be even more callous. It was tawdry, sitting here waiting for death. I couldn't save her.

Perhaps I could have saved her, long ago, if I'd done things differently.

I was sagging in my chair. I should sit up straighter. Shoulders back, stomach in, chin up. Self-conscious... who could hold this pose for long? I'll soon collapse back into me, so what's the point?

I was there, like I had always been there: helplessly dragged along at my mother's side, but useless to her. I felt like a child again. I had even stopped trying to talk to her now, out loud or in my head. I wasn't helping either of us by being there, but I still had to be there. I felt tired and confused, my thoughts running aground and listing. And still she breathed.

Tuesday

I woke, in my own bed, from a predictable dream: my mother, like a Shakespearean ghost, pointed a finger of condemnation at me and I was taken down from the dock, down the yellow back stairs into a cell, where I had to hand over my bag, my keys and my clothes, and sit naked on a nailed-down bench waiting for the van... I woke in my own bed, with my clothes and my things and the safety of my solitude.

My house is very small and very old, as if perhaps people were smaller in the old days. The whole row of cottages is one long finger of white-painted stone, like stick of nougat, and the slate-tiled roofs look too low to fit in an upper floor. Through the front door you walk right into my sitting room, almost in the middle before you've taken two steps, and an uneven archway that no door could ever fit into leads through to the kitchen. The stairs climb up the wall of the sitting room, through a dark hole to where my bedroom is hidden away beneath a lumpy, sloping ceiling that gives it the feel of a burrow. The thick stone walls conceal me from everyone.

When I betrayed my mother and left her, I went to live in a modern flat; but it was too noisy, and I felt too exposed. I used to hear pounding feet, laughter and televisions all around me, and I started to worry that they could hear me; or maybe, worse, that they couldn't hear me - maybe I was the silent girl with silent footsteps, and while everyone else in the building was bold and expanding I was shrinking and fading. I bought this old cottage thirteen years ago and I have lived quietly here ever since. It's cosy and safe and just the right size for one person.

I guessed they would have rung me in the night if she'd died, so I guessed she was still there, and we would have another day in this strange limbo. I showered and dressed, and set off just as if I was going to work, but wearing my inappropriately jolly clothes, including trainers today, because of my sore foot. Tuesday is the busiest day at work. All the cases arrested and bailed at the weekend have their first appearance on a Tuesday, in an overlisted and confused Court One, and we usually have trials taking place in Courts Two and Three at the same time. Often trials fold - because either the defendant or the witnesses fail to turn up, or because the defendant decides at the last minute to plead guilty - so one usher is assigned to deal with both courtrooms on the assumption that one will be cancelled; but you can be sure that either both courts will fold or both will go ahead, with one usher rushing between. And to top it all we have a youth court on a Tuesday too, tucked away in Court Four with the friendly chairs and the private waiting area, and the usher's job is to establish from the sullen teenage boys whether they are accompanied by anyone who could count as a parent.

My friend Emma works in the youth court; she works for the Youth Offending Team, a sort of probation service for kids, and she's one of those rare people who enjoys talking to teenagers. She has big hair and short nails and touches people on the shoulder in a way that makes them feel understood. She reminds me a bit of Mark. We occasionally have lunch together on a Tuesday if she's not too busy on her phone tracking down accommodation for a tragic teen or calming end-of-tether parents. She's tried to persuade me to come and work for the Youth Offending Team - a proper, important, satisfying job, where people depend on you - but I don't want that. I don't want that sort of job. I like having lunch with her though, because she talks a lot, telling stories and gossip with lots of gestures, nudges and comic faces. She has lots of friends, and inhuman energy levels.

I wondered how they would cope without me on a Tuesday. Perhaps it would be a lucky day and both trials would fold early.

It had rained during the night, and the rain had hung around into the morning. Everything had turned dark and earthy. People had their heads down, and as I drove through town bedraggled pedestrians kept trying to dash across in front of me. In the hospital car park the tarmac had become a landscape of miniature islands

44

and lakes, the puddles bursting into frantic circles. Even my parking ticket dampened between the machine and my hand.

My mother's eyes were wide open again, and I thought about those dolls whose eyes open when they're upright and close when they're laid flat. When I learnt that the trick is a weight inside each pivoted eye, so that as the doll moves up or back the eye stays still and level, I thought of dolls' eyes completely differently; not as opening and closing expressively but as steady, still and blind. My mother had been dressed in a once-white nightie today, with short lacy sleeves. I should have kissed her but she looked too monstrous, so instead I touched her hand, limp and dry, and sat down in my high-backed seat.

There was a new person in the bed opposite my mother. He must have come in during the night. He was sitting up in front of fat white pillows and the sheet was drawn neatly across his tummy as if he had been tucked in. His face was grey and bewildered. He was surrounded by his wife and teenaged children, all stood around the bed as if there wasn't time to sit down. His wife had long pink nails and she held her hand over her mouth, pressing her fingers up and down over her lips, then rubbing one eye, then suddenly grasping her husband's hand and leaning in to speak. She was never still and seemed perpetually startled; she was very tense. The teenaged girl was hollow-faced and crumpled, and the boy leaned back and forth against the end of the bed frame like a child swinging on railings. Both of them kept looking across at my mother, thoughtlessly at first, then furtively.

I looked away from them. I remembered Dr Amin's promise of a private room, but there was no-one to ask; the nurses were all moving around busily, striding down the corridor and conferring with each other. There was no privacy in hospital, and definitely no privacy in dying. I remembered a medical student I knew once; he was the boyfriend of my schoolfriend's older sister. He told us that in their second year at university they dissect people, real dead people who had donated their bodies to medical science. In a big, cold room there are bodies laid out on tables, and the students slowly dismantle them over a period of weeks, peeling away skin and fat and muscle, scooping out the heart and liver and eyes. He said that the dead people's faces were covered most of the time, to preserve their dignity, but I could imagine nothing less dignified than lying naked and exposed from the neck down.

In hospital, weak and helpless, we are stripped naked and handled by strangers, wheeled in and out of rooms and corridors; beds, the most intimate pieces of furniture, become stages on which we are displayed, ugly and decrepit. We all end up like this. There is no privacy in the court where I work either. As usher, I lead witnesses into the witness box. They aren't allowed into the courtroom until they are called to give their evidence, so when I lead them in they enter a large, sombre room, obstructed by heavy wooden benches and overlooked by silent watching faces; everybody has stopped speaking and waits while they find their place. I lead them to the stand where they must step up into a three-walled waist-high box, and I hand them a small thick bible and say," Repeat after me. I solemnly and sincerely swear."

"I solemnly and sincerely swear."

"That the evidence I am about to give."

"That the evidence I am about to give."

"Is the truth, the whole truth, and nothing but the truth."

"Is the truth, the whole truth, and nothing but the truth."

And then I leave them. They stand in the witness box, surrounded by faces looking at them, and not knowing who will speak first or what will be said. And then they are asked questions - formal, serious questions: name, occupation, address; where they were when it happened, who they were with. Were they drunk? Do they usually get drunk? Was it really like that? Are they sure he said that? Are they lying? Their answers are written down, every word recorded.

For the defendants it is even worse. At a sentencing hearing, the defendant sits in the dock, alone, while his solicitor stands and tells the whole room the whole sad story of his life, stripping him naked and slitting him open to show the pathetic mess inside. His wife left him, he hasn't worked in years, he has debts, drug addiction, alcohol problems, homelessness; his baby was stillborn, his mother put him in care, he was abused as a child. All the sordid

46

shame of his life is pinned up for everyone to see while his punishment is decided.

When I mention my job some people say stupid things like "Ooh, is it scary, being around all those criminals?" They don't understand that the defendants are the victims in the courtroom: they are on trial, or being sentenced; they have been caught, and all their bravado and threat has gone. They are helpless, at the mercy of the court. Often people don't understand either that many defendants are just like themselves, ordinary people, not a species apart; anyone can find themselves summoned to a magistrates court. Speeding, careless driving, overtaking at the wrong moment or risking that third pint. An argument in a pub, an argument in the street, an argument at home; a thrown plate, a punch, the police turning up. A clampdown at work and suddenly taking home offcuts or stationery isn't a perk, it's theft; a lie to help a friend, a clever tax form, an exaggerated insurance claim - well, everyone does it, don't they? We had a man in a suit who had thumped a teenager he caught jumping on his car; that's assaulting a minor, a schedule one offence, very serious. We had an old woman who hated her neighbour and shouted at her over the garden wall every time she went outside to hang her washing; that's harassment, maximum two years. We had a man who didn't tell the taxman he was renting out his flat; a girl who didn't see a cyclist and drove into him; a woman who poured wine over the head of her husband's mistress. All of them were shocked to be in a courtroom, as if some surreal misunderstanding had sent them to the wrong destination, like luggage sent to Helsinki or a train diverted to the moon. All of them had to sit alone while their story was read out, the magistrates frowned and the court reporter scribbled.

My mother was still breathing, as if she would never stop. I sat and looked at her, but with so many people in the ward I couldn't speak to her, even inside my head, so I sat silently, apart from her, in my chair with the high back. Perhaps just sitting was enough; perhaps that was all that was required of me. Mark used to say that sometimes the simple presence of another human being is a comfort. I wondered if it would be rude if I looked at my phone. I thought about how awful it would look if I sat scrolling through celebrities 'make-up tips and pictures of kittens at my mother's bedside, waiting for her to die. Maybe if I read news stories out loud to her that would appear caring, and it would fill the time. Reading out loud would be tiring, though, and perhaps too strange. People would look at me, and listen. I don't like people to look at me, or listen. At work I like being the usher, a human signpost - no-one looks me in the face. I couldn't bear to be a lawyer, addressing the court with all eyes on me; or a magistrate, up on the stage.

I was hoping my mother would be moved to a private room, where I would have more silence in which to spread out.

I have always craved privacy. When we lived in Lucas Street, I would sit on my bed in the evenings, in the centre of the room, reading or drawing or playing with my little dolls, and if I heard my mother creaking up the stairs I would freeze and hold my breath and wait; sometimes she went into the toilet, flicked on the light and slammed the bolt, and I could breathe again, but sometimes she came right up to my room, tapping the door as she came through it, restless and bored, sitting on my bed and making my drawings slide and my felt tips roll into the folds of the duvet. "What are you doing?" she'd sigh. "Come down and talk to me. What are you doing up here on your own? Don't be so boring."

After the fire we moved into Willow House, and there we had to share a room, and even a bed. It was a B&B, but not the sort you go to on holiday. It was Temporary Accommodation. We had new things, because everything had been lost in the fire: new clothes, new shoes, new pencil case, new hairbands; it felt to me that these belongings were temporary, too, belonging to Willow House and not to me.

Willow House was a big Victorian town house with fancy gables and finials and even a forbidden turret with a pointed roof, and inside it was tall and creaky, divided into odd shaped rooms and unexpected doors. We lived in room number six, up the first flight of stairs, and to get up them you had to press a light switch that was a fat round button at the bottom of the stairs, and then race up before the timer gave out and the light clicked off. I was terrified of being outrun by the darkness and several times I almost tumbled

48

up the stairs. Our room was large and square, with two long, thin windows, barred at the bottom to stop children falling out, and a ceiling edged with plaster curls like swirls of ice cream. There was a double bed, which was high, and as soft as a pillow, so that we rolled into one another in the night, and a chest of drawers carved from such thick wood that the drawers themselves were tiny on the inside; they got stuck if you opened them more than two inches. There was a washbasin, an odd, mushroom-coloured thing, in the corner, like a piece of bathroom that had been misplaced. Above it hung a mirror with a long straight crack down the middle, and when I cleaned my teeth I bent my head hastily to spit out, afraid that the mirror would see its chance to split and crash down on my head.

Our belongings, meagre as they were, began to accumulate on the floor, so we were soon knee-deep in clothes, shoes and bags, searching for lost things and irritably blaming each other for the mess. Sometimes we "tidied up" by gathering random items into piles, creating apparent order; but when I looked for my homework I had to thumb through stacks of magazines, bills, solicitors 'letters, torn envelopes, borrowed books and money off vouchers. I tried to keep my clothes orderly in a sports bag, but over time they swirled together into a clump of t-shirts and socks and I would dig vainly for the skirt I'd seen only the day before. It was as if all our things were swirling around us in perpetual movement, just as we ourselves were only passing through, moving along on our journey without destination.

The people in Willow House also accumulated in random, ever-shifting clumps, in the dining room downstairs in the morning or evening. The dining room was the only communal space, apart from the two unspeakable bathrooms, although some residents would sometimes wander into the kitchen - and some staff would sometimes allow it - and gossip or whisper or grant access to the fridge - while other staff on another day might raise their voices in horror that the 'Private 'sign had been transgressed. Willow House was a place of strict but fluctuating rules. There was an atmosphere that similarly alternated between sleepy apathy and violent outbursts. Some people were friends and then they were enemies, and then they were friends again; some people stayed for one night and some people stayed forever; some people were tumultuous, crying in the kitchen or shouting over the bannisters, and some people came and went quietly and no-one ever even knew their name. Some people didn't speak English, but you couldn't always tell, because some people who did speak English would just stare vacantly if they were spoken to; and some people never spoke at all.

We had to vacate Willow House during the day. It was one of the rules: between ten am and four pm the residents were shut out. Another rule was that we all had to be in by ten pm; after that the Yale lock was dropped and if you were out you couldn't get back in until the morning. Sometimes people would come home late, drunk, and shout at the windows and throw up in the garden. One night a window was smashed and the police came. Another time someone got into trouble for letting someone else in after ten. There was also a rule that residents weren't allowed in each other's rooms, but my mum said half the women were shagging half the men. Some people propped their doors open and sat together companionably in the corridors, on the floor with their legs stretched across the hallway, playing music and drinking from cans. There was a rule of No Alcohol so people held the cans under their jackets. There was a rule of No Smoking so people leaned out of their windows to smoke, and ran off laughing if staff came looking. Little flat cigarette ends were trampled into the weeds and gravel of the garden. The staff stood outside the back door to smoke, scowling and muttering and fizzing their cigarette ends into an old pot full of rainwater. Once I looked at them too long and a fat woman shouted something at me; I couldn't make out what it was but the other woman laughed.

My mum and I didn't eat in the dining room. The only meal provided was breakfast, when the staff slammed down cereal boxes and bottles of milk; the cereal was mostly stale because no-one sealed the boxes properly and clots of dried food were stuck to the spoons. Sometimes someone would be drunk from the night before, or someone would be crying, or drying their hair at one of the sockets, or sitting on the table with their boots on a chair. In the evenings people sometimes brought takeaways into the dining room because there was a rule of No Food in our rooms, but the staff would complain about curry crushed into the carpet and no-one would clean it up. My mum bought a secret kettle for our room and we made soups and pot noodles, and experimented with cooking pasta by leaving it to stand in a mug of boiled water; I came to like it, chewy in the middle, coated with slimy starch and topped with tomato ketchup. We became experts in foods that didn't need refrigeration or cooking: peanut butter sandwiches, marmite sandwiches, tinned sweetcorn with vinegar, cold beans with vinegar. For breakfast we ate sticky cereal bars and black tea.

We had a great summer, though, that summer of "staying out" every day, because we had to. My mother wasn't working and I was on holiday from school and we were let loose, with nowhere to be and nothing to do. That summer is vivid in my memory. Holiday memories are overwritten by photographs, but that summer was unrecorded and remains pure in my mind as a jumble of images and feelings. We sat in cafés reading magazines, skimming pictures of unwearable fashion and untenable celebrities while our pots of tea grew cold and stewed; we ate chips and ice cream in the park, on our favourite bench overlooking the tennis courts, watching the serious children taking turns to swing their racquets as their instructor showed them; we tried on outfits we would never buy, taking the maximum bundle of garments into the changing rooms and giggling at each other in frocks and blouses.

It was that summer that my mother started shoplifting, from boredom as much as need. I would wait down the street for her to come out, elated, and flash me a glimpse of whatever she had pinched: a chocolate bar, a cheap necklace, a bottle of purple nail polish. My favourite was a unicorn hair clip she gave me that twinkled pink and blue, and I wore it every day, sometimes forgetting to take it out at bedtime and finding it, tangled and painful, in my hair the next morning.

I had grown too old for toys, but I had just one: a Polly Pocket set inside a small, hard plastic purse, like a make-up case, which I could carry about with me. When I opened it up, the inside was a little house for two tiny plastic girls; the tiny rooms were beautifully detailed, with moulded beds, dressing tables and kitchen appliances, and each room was decorated with wallpaper and pictures and false windows showing a sunny garden outside. I loved to shut up the little house and know that the dolls were safely hidden away in their own little world.

We had to leave Willow House at the end of the summer. It was Temporary Accommodation and people weren't supposed to stay long, in case it began to feel permanent. It was like one of those relationships that you agree at the outset is just a fling: if one person starts to get serious, the other must immediately end it. We bundled up all our haphazard belongings and moved to Cross Street. The house at Cross Street was also Victorian, but smaller, a four-bedroomed family house converted into a shared house for strangers. We had the biggest room, with two single beds and a wardrobe, only it wasn't really a bedroom: it had been the sitting room of the house, on the ground floor, with a bay window overlooking the street. We had to stuff the window with net curtains to preserve our privacy, and even then we were caught between the voices of passers-by in the street outside and the voices of other tenants in the kitchen next door.

It was a friendlier place than Willow House, though, and there was a communal kitchen linked by an arch to a communal dining room, and two of the tenants had been there a long time. There was Darren, who had pink hair and sometimes cooked a meal for everyone, and Lisa, who was a part-time student and part-time barmaid. She had the bedroom in the attic, with a fire escape outside her window, and I longed to sit out on it with her. The other two rooms were never occupied for long, and we had a series of strange housemates: noisy people, mad people, people who didn't wash up and people who didn't come home. It was a house of young people, my mother said, and she decided she liked being around young people.

It was strange to see her looking so old in a hospital bed. Her hair was greasy and twisted, her jaw slack, and the flesh of her face hung strangely. She looked small, too, as if she had shrunk, and the thin bedclothes were raised only feebly by the vague shape of her. She looked as if she was already dead. A terrible thing. It must be terrible for people who are terminally ill, seeing in the eyes of those around them that they are already half gone. It was shocking that I was sitting there, waiting for her to die.

When we first arrived at Cross Street, it was new and cold, and the nights were made of new sounds and smells, and although we had twin beds I used to crawl in with her when it was dark. "Aw, you're too big now," she would say, but she always let me stay. She cuddled me.

The macaroni cheese in the hospital canteen was stringy and dried up at the edges, brown and crusty. I still like my pasta underdone, the way we made it in Willow House when we only had a kettle, by cooking it in slowly cooling water: pasta with a hard core, a dark ridge running through it. I suppose my tastes were baked hard in childhood, like those lottery winners who still eat beans on toast and import marmite to eat on their Caribbean islands. I suppose we all carry our childhoods inside us, our child selves remaining forever at our core.

There was a queue at the till. The woman in front of me, buying enormous baguette sandwiches balanced across small plates, was saying:" It was supposed to be a heatwave this week," and the woman behind the till, studying her drawer of coins and carefully picking one from each compartment to produce the right change, snorted and said:" Probably down south it is. They only give the forecast for London." Then the woman behind me in the queue tossed in:" I think it's later in the week, the heatwave, from Thursday they said," and I found myself enclosed in a circle of convivial weather-talk, the only silent one, the cuckoo in the nest. I could think of nothing to say and I tried smiling and nodding; but that made me feel even more like an outsider, an alien, a misfit failing at the simplest of human bonding rituals. I paid for my macaroni cheese and coffee with my phone and shuffled away.

I sat alone near the rain-obscured window. Outside I could see an unfamiliar and streaky view of houses strewn unevenly up a hillside towards an oversized church. It was probably a village once, before it was engulfed by the spreading city. The sky was grey with rain and I thought for a moment about aeroplanes flying above it, in another world where it was still blue. Then someone came and sat at a table between me and the window, so I could no longer look out. I should go back to my mother's bedside. I sat and finished my cold coffee.

She was still alive, and the ward was quiet.

"Hello, Mum, I'm back. I had macaroni cheese."

I wondered if she remembered the way we ate pasta at Willow House, but even if she had been conscious I couldn't have formulated the question. Especially if she had been conscious. We had long ago lost the bond of reminiscence, and the past was only spoken about to score points. Our common history was just a store of ammunition. "You dragged me around like you were having a second youth," I said to her once.

"You're a selfish bitch," I said to her.

"You think everything's about you," I said to her. "You never loved me. You've never loved anyone."

"You're beyond selfish," she said to me. "You're completely hard, cold as ice. Deceitful as a snake. A snake you are, cold-blooded and venomous."

She had boyfriends, of course, before Mark. There was Craig, who was younger than her; and Dave, who was older; and Warren, who had a ponytail. Craig rode dirt bikes, and we spent Saturdays watching him buzzing up and down muddy pits. When he took his helmet off his neck was pink and raw from acne and shaving rash. Dave had lots of mates and he came to visit us in Cross Street in different cars with different hangers-on, who would sit in a line on my bed like birds on a telephone wire, each with a can of beer, sniggering at a joke. My mother didn't go out with either Craig or Dave for very long. Her relationships were an amusement, like a TV series you might get into for a while. "I think I might give him the flick," she'd say, contentedly. "I think his time's up." Sometimes she got drunk and told me my father was the only man she'd ever loved.

In the dining room at Cross Street, she would sit at the table opposite our housemate Lisa and smoke and chat as if they were the same age; late at night, if I came down for a glass of water, they were sometimes sitting with a bottle of wine between them, talking about men. It made them feel bohemian to invite me to join them.

They used a white saucer as an ashtray and I remember the smoky brown circles that marked it and the perfect cylinders of ash that crumbled at a breath. Lisa had a boyfriend called Paul, tall and tousle-haired, who stood awkwardly in the kitchen sometimes, his fingers squashed into the taut pockets of his jeans, waiting for her to get ready. She enjoyed telling my mother about Paul's harebrained projects. Like a puppy, he was forever bounding enthusiastically at one idea or the next: potholing, antique dealing, Christianity. Sometimes his enthusiasms involved other women, like the anarchist meetings he went to with Caroline. "He keeps trying not to talk about Caroline," Lisa said, flicking her ash with a wry smile. "It's such a crush." As a part-time barmaid and part-time student Lisa was both worldly-wise and intellectual, street smart and book smart at the same time. She was a small, big-haired young woman. "It's okay," she said of Paul. "He's like Mr Benn, you know, always trying on new hats. He'll always come back to Festive Road."

My mother explained to me that *Mr Benn* was a kids' TV show from years ago, and in every episode Mr Benn tried on an outfit that took him off on a magical adventure: a knight's suit of armour transported him to the middle ages, a clown's nose to a circus and a sheriff's badge to the wild west. At the end of each episode, though, he always came back to his house in Festive Road. I liked the neat psychological analogy, and, for the first time, listening to Lisa, I realised that you could tame people with psychology. If another tenant exploded in temper at the state of the kitchen, Lisa would raise her eyebrows and whisper "OCD"; if someone played their music deliberately loud she would call them passive-aggressive. Of my mother's boyfriends she sagely declared Craig to be immature and Dave to be needy, insecure and probably gay.

Still, it took some time before it occurred to me that the key to my mother could be found in psychology. When the idea clicked, I started to seek out self-help books, pseudoscientific popular paperbacks and hardcore medical encyclopaedias, sometimes in libraries, sometimes in bookshops, where I would kneel on the floor and rummage intensely though the text for clues to my mother; later, I poked about the internet, following links down rabbit holes to muddy medical research papers and websites flashing ads for liposuction. It was fascinating how psychiatric conditions came in and out of fashion, even changing their names and shifting between groupings of sub-conditions and associated conditions.

My mother was complicated, and promising paths petered out like fox trails in the woods. Histrionic Personality Disorder: attention seeking, dramatic, manipulative... the patient craves excitement and lacks consideration for others... but is also an exhibitionist, desperate to impress, a description that didn't suit my mother at all. Borderline Personality Disorder: attention seeking, unstable in relationships, reckless, self-damaging behaviour... but depression and anxiety were difficult to fit with my mother's apparent confidence. Bipolar Disorder: periods of mania, feeling energetic and restless, and periods of low mood and hopelessness; but my mother didn't swing from one to the other - she seemed to experience both at the same time. She was so big and complicated and unpredictable that she didn't fit the labels or comply with the rubric; diagnosing her was like trying to pack water into a suitcase. Perhaps doctors always have this problem, following a meandering path of funny feelings and strange aches and itches and rashes that lead nowhere. Or perhaps there was nothing wrong with her.

Narcissistic Personality Disorder: egocentricity, vanity, lack of empathy, superficial in relationships. Dysphoria: a profound sense of unease or dissatisfaction and agitation. Kleptomania: an urge to steal, perhaps a branch of obsessive compulsive disorder. Adult ADHD: impulsiveness, restlessness, hyperactivity.

At school we read the folk tale of the blind men and the elephant. Six blind men encounter an elephant and each feels a different part of it: one feels the trunk and declares it to be a snake, one feels the tail and says it's a rope, and so on. It struck me that psychology was like that: the mind is so vast and chaotic that you could look at one set of characteristics and label it OCD, or look at another set and find schizoid personality disorder.

When she finally, and suddenly, came to the attention of psychiatrists, it was actually a shock for me. It was like quarrelling with a neighbour for years, trading the same old insults and complaints, shouted over the fence, back and forth, only for the police to turn up one day and arrest everybody. I remember sitting tightly in Mark's car as we drove to the hospital. I could see his knee raise and lower as he changed gear, his knuckles tautening his skin as he squeezed the gearstick, his eyes moving from the road ahead to the mirror and back. At a junction he leaned forward in his seatbelt and hugged the steering wheel, while the loud ticking of the indicator interrupted our talk. At the hospital we were told that she had been taken to Acorn Ward, and that she was being assessed. We joked that the doctors didn't know what they were letting themselves in for: "*She ll* be assessing *them!*" Mark said.

We stood outside the ward.

"She'll be fine," he said. "Of course she'll be fine. Your mother is one of life's survivors." I was trembling slightly, despite myself: it felt like a reckoning had come. Although I had thought for years that she was mad, I couldn't believe my mother was actually in a psychiatric ward, that her edifice had crashed down." She'll be fine. She'll be demanding to come home!" he said. "She'll be up and stomping about by now."

I nodded. "I know my rights!" I exclaimed, imitating her voice, or at least imitating what she would say, for my voice was high and pinched. Mark laughed broadly.

I hadn't really believed she would ever be taken away by psychiatrists.

Back at Cross Street, Mr Benn didn't, in the end, come back to Festive Road. Paul left Lisa, and in fact ended up at New Gaia with us. But that's a whole other story.

The hospital shop reminded me of motorway service stations: there was the same erratic mix of necessities and useless gifts. There were tissues, aspirin and even underpants; floral wash bags and odd embarrassing items aimed at the elderly; flowers and brooches and mugs for 'the best gran in the world'; newspapers and magazines and plastic toys to keep children quiet. There was an astonishingly shameless display of sweets, crisps and chocolate. I found that I had wandered over to the magazines. The tabloid newspapers were shouting their outraged and truncated headlines at me, the 'men's interest 'section was all cars and yachts and coarse fishing, and 'women's interests 'were apparently real-life stories of rape, crocheting made easy and the diet secrets of television presenters.

My mum and I used to enjoy reading magazines together, laughing at the vacuous articles and unlikely fashions:£" 350 for that!"

"Listen to this," Mum would say, and adopt a falsely excited voice to read out a fawning interview with a celebrity who managed to juggle fame, motherhood and designing the interior of her beautiful Kensington home.

I didn't buy a magazine, but set off back to Marlowe Ward through the colour-coded maze of corridors. I'd noticed that the wards in the vicinity of Marlowe Ward were named Jonson Ward, Peele Ward and Dekker Ward - they were all named after Elizabethan playwrights. There was no Shakespeare Ward, though; perhaps he was too famous and would have elevated one ward far above the others, so they had decided to name the wards after Elizabethan Playwrights Who Aren't Shakespeare. I googled Christopher Marlowe: born 1564, died 1593, stabbed to death in a fight in a pub. He was believed to have been a government spy and he was arrested on various occasions for involvement in libel, murder and counterfeiting; he was scandalously an atheist and less scandalously a homosexual. His most famous play was *Dr Faustus*, about a man who sold his soul to the devil, believing he could trick his way out of the deal by repenting just before death. Of course it didn't work out for him and at the end of the play he can only wait for death to come for him. Demons arrive and delightedly drag him away to hell.

I put my phone away and pressed the buzzer to be let back into Marlowe Ward.

My mother was still there, still breathing like ragged bellows, and I realised that I was becoming used to her in this state, so that it would be a shock, now, when she died. I was used to the wards, the corridor, my chair and my routine of meals and coffees. Human beings become so quickly accustomed to new situations; we wear in more quickly than a pair of shoes.

"Hi, Mum, I'm back."

"Oh, you're still here, are you?"

"Yeah. Of course I am."

Years ago, when we first moved into Cross Street, my mum had an old friend who was diagnosed with cancer, and we went to visit her. I was terrified. When we got there, though, it was an ordinary house, full of her kids 'ordinary things - she said they were at their dad's for the weekend - and the woman looked ordinary, although she moved slowly around the kitchen when she made us a cup of tea. There were no medical machines in the house, no oxygen cylinders or tablets or wheelchairs; the cancer was all on the inside. I didn't want to drink from the cup she gave me, so I just held it, listening to grown up talk, until it went cold. Afterwards, out in the fresh air, my mum said "God, I don't want to go like that. That's not for me. Give me a heart attack or a stroke or a car crash; I want to be gone like *that* -" and she clicked her fingers, snap. I was terrified of her dying, back then: she was my everything, and I loved her more than I've ever loved anyone. There was a news story around that time about a little girl who saved her mother's life by dialling 999, and I played that story over and over in my head: my mother would have a heart attack and I would call an ambulance, and they would jolt her chest and smile and say," Yes! She's breathing. She'll be fine, thanks to you."

I used to worry about her, sometimes, when she was back late. She often went for a night out. I'd do my homework, cross legged on my bed, while she was getting ready, dabbing her eyeshadow, spraying perfume or pinching smoothing cream into her hair; and then when she was gone I'd huddle down under my duvet and watch our little TV. It was a cosy solitude, sometimes enhanced by a multipack of cheese and onion crisps that I would carefully apportion to myself at half hourly intervals, and as the curtain grew dark the room was lit only by a dull bedside lamp and the bright dancing screen. I would snuggle lower into my bed as it got later and later. My mum was usually home by eleven, but sometimes it got to midnight, and I would have to reassure myself by thinking about missed buses, unreliable taxis and all the other times that it had got to midnight and she had been fine.

One night, she came back quite late, apologised for being "a bit sozzled" and wobbled off to the bathroom to clean her teeth. I extinguished the TV and curled up. When she came back, she clicked off the lamp and got into her bed with a sigh, turning over a few times like a dog trying to get comfortable, and then she got up again, without putting the lamp on, and came over to sit heavily on my bed.

"Can I talk to you?" she whispered, breathing toothpaste and wine.

I propped myself up on one elbow.

"I need to tell someone," she went on. "I've been seeing Paul." She paused. She sounded excited, not ashamed. "Do you think I'm bad?"

I could never think she was bad, and I reassured her accordingly.

"Lisa doesn't know, the silly little cow. He'd leave her for me in a flash. I don't want him to, though, he's just a kid." Her voice was thick and slow, sticking to some of the words. "What am I like? I bet it's no more than your dad gets up to." She laughed, and flopped back on to her own bed, as if laughing was exhausting. She fell asleep on top of the covers and started to snore.

My dad had "access" to me, which meant he would pick me up on one designated Saturday a month and take me out for lunch. He pulled his smooth company car into a space down the street and waited for me, fiddling with his air conditioning. "Tell him you've no shoes for school," my mum would be saying. "Tell him the price of that bloody PE kit." She had chosen my clothes for my performance: I had to look poor. It was true that we had very little money, but that just made it all the more important that I didn't unwittingly give an impression of comfort. My dad drove me out to the American Diner on the ring road, or the pizza place next to the multiscreen cinema; we walked across big car parks bordered with scrubby bushes and ordered from glossy menus. My drinks were fizzy and heavy with ice cubes, and I ate garlic bread, cajun chicken, pizza triangles made soggy by coleslaw or sticky sweet ribs that stained my fingers. My dad ate quickly, then pushed back his seat and sat with one ankle balanced on the other knee, his foot jiggling, while he scrolled through texts on his phone. While I sweated through a syrupy dessert he went outside to make calls, and I could see him pacing, laughing into his phone and pulling faces at the ground.

His job title was Product Development Manager, but Mum said he was "a bloody salesman". He worked for a company that made electronic components. "I only wish I could have you over to stay," he'd say, "but my flat's the size of a box; honestly, it's just a room with a toilet. I can barely afford that. I only turn the heating on when it snows. The car's not mine, you know, it's a company car." He always pointed that out, every time I saw him. Everything he owned was really the company's, from his phone to his clothes. His image of success was deliberately created by the company for their own ends, as a king might dress his footmen in gold to impress his visitors.

When I came home, I reported on the cheesecake or profiteroles, and then my mum's mouth would twitch into a knowing smile as she asked, quietly: "And is he still.... expanding?"

It always set us giggling. It was true that he was putting on weight, steadily and irrefutably. His shirts were still tucked into his belted trousers but the trousers were widening and the belts were more and more hidden by his swelling belly, and his face was changing as the bones became submerged like rocks at high tide.

"Is he any... broader?"

I giggled. "A bit chunky."

"Another notch on the belt?"

"A bit tubby."

"A fat cat."

My mum had jobs. She worked for a while at a newsagents, but when the owner's son came back from college there were fewer and fewer hours available. Lisa got her some shifts at the pub where she worked, but the noise and the heat were exhausting and the tills infuriatingly irrational, and she swore she wouldn't do another night there if they paid her double. She did some telesales for a while but the shifts were all over the place and the bus journey took nearly an hour. She had an old friend who was doing reflexology; her eldest had gone away to university and she had set up a treatment room in a spare bedroom, with proper equipment and pot plants. "I could have done something like that," my mum said, bitterly, "if we still had a proper life, and a proper home." It was late at night and she was crying. "How did I end up like this? Fucking down-and-outs, we are, scraping around at the bottom."

Over the winter she had been shoplifting gloves. She had sharp-smelling leather ones in different colours, and woollen ones with furry cuffs or sequins. I had red ones, pink ones, grey ones and stripy ones; fingerless gloves, and fingerless gloves with a little hood to fold over the fingers, and mittens with fleecy insides and kitten faces on the backs. "Enough gloves for a centipede!" my mum laughed. "I must be a right nutcase." I only had one coat, though, and that was last year's: it was tight across my back, and my wrists stuck out like white bones when I reached forwards. In the summer she took to pinching make-up, and we had a hundred shades of unused lipstick. I had a zip-up wash bag to take with me between our room and the bathroom; it was a spotty plastic bag, small but sturdy enough to stand chunkily on its own, and my mother brought home fancy shampoo and conditioner, straightening creme and finishing spritz, and skin reviver and toner and buttery cleanser, all in elegant little jars and tubes that I carefully packed upright in my bag, using a facecloth like bubblewrap to support them.

The shared bathroom at Cross Street became a special place for me, and my memory of it is a carefully packed parcel too, a memory I can unwrap and immerse myself in, almost as if the place still exists and I can visit it. Although the bathroom was shared, there was a bolt to slide across on the door, and once it was locked the room became completely my own, the one private place in the house. I pulled the brown string that set the extractor fan rattling, and turned the taps so that water crashed into the deep, old-fashioned bath. There might be a shampoo bottle on the side, congealed and abandoned, untouched by everyone in the belief that it belonged to someone else; there might be a grubby cloth, dried out and stiff, left behind from someone's resentful attempt at cleaning; there might be black mould in the recess of the window, and a crack in the frosted glass itself, and the corners of the room might be furred with dust and hair and the ceiling yellow and speckled; but it was private, my own solitary space for half an hour, and I felt completely invisible in the soft steamy mist. Undressed, I stepped into the deep, warm water that made a hollow, gulping sound as I sloshed about and settled in. When I lay back, the water slowed in its swirling and fell silent, and I imagined that one day I would have my own house, with my own locked front door, and I would sit in my own bath, with the whole world locked outside.

Sometimes someone would rap on the bathroom door or shake the handle. "Someone in there?" I didn't want to answer and reveal myself to be sitting naked in the tub. I would splash the water a little, moving my knees so the water rolled heavily across them with a groan, and then I would wait, anonymously, for the person to go away.

At Willow House my mother used to warn me to "watch out for the bloody perverts", and always enter and leave the bathroom fully dressed, although many of the adults there wandered about in dressing gowns or drunkenly in pants. At Cross Street, too, we had transient co-tenants and my mother would casually remark," Watch out for that new guy," without further explanation. I wore my school uniform as protection, as uniforms are: it hid me, and designated me a schoolgirl, out of bounds. I felt safe in my uniform.

The last time I saw my mother, when we met in a cafe, she was wearing that green leather coat like it was a uniform. At the time I didn't think about it, but I remember now that she didn't take it off even though the cafe was warm. It was a vintage coat, unusual, smart but casual, timeless, a coat that marked her as non-conformist. She sat at the table fidgeting with her unlit cigarette, twitching her mouth and sending her eyes on restless scouting missions around the room, and her acceptably eccentric coat both hid her and explained her, and allowed her to go about her business in her own slightly strange way.

We spoke about Mark that day.

"Have you seen him?" she asked.

"No, of course not," I said. "Have you?"

The fact that she asked me indicated that she hadn't seen him; unless it was some kind of double bluff. We scowled at each other.

"Of course I haven't seen him," she said, almost ripping her unlit and creased cigarette. "How could I ever see him again, after what you did?"

The hospital ward smelled of gravy this afternoon, and women in sand-coloured tabards were clearing away plates and handing out cups of tea. The tea was brought to the beds in cups balanced on saucers; they were proper, institutional tea cups, sturdy china in a dull grey-green like the British sea, the sort of cups that would have been rattled out in a field hospital at Dunkirk or raised to soft, wobbling lips in an overheated nursing home. They were tea cups that belonged with numbered prison blankets and the smell of disinfectant.

Two nurses came bustling in, just as I was adrift in contemplation of the tea cups, to tell me that a single room had come available for my mother and they were moving her right now. "Good to have a bit of privacy, eh?" enthused the bigger nurse, and she pushed her way round the bed, unplugging and unclipping and untucking. She was a big, confident woman, the kind of person who comes at you like a bowling ball, and her companion was a quiet, foreign nurse who didn't look at me at all but made occasional quick comments in a jargon or accent I didn't understand. They disconnected the whole bed from the room, shifted my chair after I had swiftly jumped out of it, and then wheeled the bed out through the door. It lurched and swerved slightly, like an unwieldy shopping trolley. "Mind out!" the big nurse called cheerfully to no-one in particular, and I followed them out into the corridor, not knowing where we going and afraid of being left behind.

"Here we go!" The single room had a narrower door and the bed had to be shunted back and forth to make the turn. I had to stand in the corridor while the bed and the two nurses arranged themselves in the room. There was swishing and clicking and a brief exchange of words and then the foreign nurse came out swiftly, without looking at me. I went in.

64

It was a small room with a sink. On the other side of the bed was a window, showing only sky. "This is better, isn't it?" The nurse was still bustling about, rearranging the bedcovers almost lovingly. "Much quieter. You won't be disturbed here at all." She had plump hands, and wrists that were crusted with pink eczema. "You can have some peace." She smiled across at me from the other side of the bed. "Are you on your own, love?"

Her tone had changed: she evidently had two professional voices, a solid, efficiency voice and a liquid, sympathetic one. Both voices were caring and supportive, but while the solid voice herded people and obstacles briskly, the liquid voice carried them gently and patiently. "Are you looking after yourself? Have you had something to eat?"

I reassured her that I had, and I felt myself blushing at her assumptions about me.

"That's good, you do need to look after yourself." She was nodding. "Don't you have any other family?"

I shook my head, although the thought now caught there that I should give my dad a ring to tell him what had happened. I would have to call him when she died, anyway, and he might then think it odd that I hadn't rung him sooner. I had again the awkward feeling that there was some sort of etiquette to all this next-of-kin business, and I was trampling over the flower beds and opening the wrong gates. Not only was I meant to be crying at the bedside and forgetting to eat; I should also be ringing through her address book and gathering friends and family like a muezzin calling the faithful to prayer.

The quiet foreign nurse had come back into the room behind me, and she circled the bed, clutching a cumbersome bundle of plastic and fabric. "We're going to give her a wash now," the big nurse announced, reverting back to her solid voice. They began to unwrap disposable gloves. "Why don't you go and get yourself a coffee?"

I went back out into the corridor and left my mother to be washed by strangers. They didn't shut the door but drew the thin curtain just far enough.

65

I set off purposefully to find a quiet corner, fingering the smooth edges of my phone and wondering if my dad's number was in it.

I only had his landline number. I expected him to be out, but he answered after six rings.

"Hello?"

"Hi, Dad, it's me. Amelia."

"Oh… hi, this is a nice surprise, only we've got people here…"

"I'm ringing because I've got news."

"News?"

"I've got bad news. About Mum. She's had a stroke and she's in hospital."

"What, a stroke?" I could hear a baby babbling in the background. My dad was a grandfather now - one of my half-siblings had married and produced offspring. I knew only that the baby was called Felix or Frodo or something, and my dad was very excited about it. "A stroke?"

"Yes, a stroke. She's… well, it's, you know, it's serious."

"Oh God, I'm sorry, are you okay? A stroke, bloody hell. Listen, can I put Kate on for a minute? I've got Felix in my arms." I could hear him saying something to Kate. There was a crush of indistinct voices, far away from me but brought close to my ear. Then Kate's voice came out of the crowd to speak to me.

"Amy? Oh, I'm so sorry… are you okay? Are you at the hospital?"

I confirmed that I was and tried to explain what was happening. "It's okay, she's peaceful and everything, but they don't expect her to get better, I mean, they don't think she'll keep breathing much longer, but it's okay, I mean, it's awful, but, anyway, I thought I should just let you and Dad know."

"Is there anything we can do?" Kate asked. I could hear other voices behind her.

"No, no, don't worry."

My dad's voice returned. "Sorry about that. Are you okay? Let me know if you need anything, won't you? It's a shock, isn't it? Do let me know if there's any change, won't you? You've got this number. It's a shock, isn't it?"

I agreed it was a shock and said goodbye, and as he said goodbye I could hear Kate asking him warmly if he was alright. I looked at my phone and ended the call.

When I got back to my mother's single room the curtain was still pulled across, just inside the open doorway, so I waited in the corridor. I had to step aside for a bulky medicines trolley, and step aside again for a cheerful porter delivering a patient on a bed. The patient's paperwork - files and x-rays - were piled up on her legs, and she was trying to make conversation with the porter from her supine position, just like a customer at the hairdressers, head back and neck cupped by the scoop in the sink, chatting to the teenager spraying hot water in her ears. I had to step aside again for a maintenance man wheeling out a dead computer.

Suddenly the curtain was whisked away and the big nurse saw me and smiled. "Did you enjoy your coffee?" she asked, briskly gathering up the things on the bed. "There, all clean now. All done." The foreign nurse slipped out past me and I went in. My mother was re-arranged and dressed in a mint green nightgown, her arms on top of the neatly drawn sheets.

"Now then." The big nurse was looking at my mother now, thoughtfully, and we both stood there, looking at her. Her eyes were half closed and pink-rimmed; her mouth was half open and made a faint gurgling sound at the end of each snore. "Now then." The nurse hugged her bundle. "Now, I can see from the notes that we gave her some painkillers when she first came in, but she hasn't been given anything since. I was wondering if we should give her some morphine." She tilted her head, like a dog does when it's puzzled. "Do you think she's in pain?"

I hadn't for a moment begun to consider the possibility that she might be in pain. How could I have not thought that she might be in pain? I hadn't really thought about her at all.

"I don't know," I said, and my voice sounded frightened. "What do you think?"

How can you tell if someone is in pain, if they can't move or speak? She was still alive in there somewhere. I had been thinking of her as a receded consciousness, reduced to a creature without thoughts, but no-one really knows what becomes of a person when the brain is fragmented. She might be drifting through a faraway dream; she might have no thoughts at all; or she might be aware of herself but trapped, paralysed, unable to scream. It was the stuff of nightmares. "I think she might be in pain," I added, and the nurse was nodding. "I think she should have painkillers." Was I so responsible for her? Did I get to decide whether she had medication or not - whether she was left in pain or saved? Was it up to me? The nurse was nodding. It really was the stuff of nightmares.

"Yes," she said, "I'll get one of the doctors to sign for an injection of morphine."

She went out. I realised that it would take time for the morphine to be prescribed: there would be a procedure, paperwork, an appropriately qualified doctor to be found, and medication to be brought from the hospital pharmacy on the other side of the building. At court we have a bureaucracy of warrants, bail sheets, summonses and committal papers; and signatures needed for a prisoner to be detained or released. "You'll have to wait," I tell anxious faces. "Take a seat."

There was no chair in the new room. I had been standing for quite some time, noticing that something was wrong but not identifying what it was. I had nowhere to sit. Could I go back into the bigger room for my chair? I was sure that the nurses wouldn't expect me to stand. There was just enough space between the door and the bed for my big, high backed chair. I had seen other people confidently dragging chairs around at visiting time, even from room to room, so I set off decisively down the corridor; it was only when I got to the door of the old room that it occurred to me that my mother's bed might have been replaced by a newcomer, and I might have been replaced, too, by a new shocked relative, pinned into my chair. I sidled into the room, feeling like a trespasser. Fortunately there was still a wide empty space where my mother's bed had been, and my big chair facing the space.

I couldn't bear to make a scraping noise, so I had to carry the bulky chair, in short heaves, lifting it in front of me and leaning back to balance the weight, trotting forward several steps and then setting it down to get my breath back and rest my arms. It was so large I had to stretch my neck to see round it, so I didn't bump into anyone, and once or twice one of the legs poked my shin painfully. Up close it smelt of warm vinyl and tart disinfectant. I felt like an ant, committed to doggedly lugging a cumbersome load for my own esoteric purposes. Fortunately no-one took any interest in me. When I got to the door of my mother's new room I banged the chair against the jamb and felt the jarring judder in my spine. It was a relief to finally drop the chair into its new position and drop myself into it.

I sat and looked at my mother in the mint green nightdress, her eyes fixed inside the thick, still lids. It was the stuff of nightmares. I remembered the last time I saw her, in the café, in the green leather coat. I saw her then as a big green dragon, a monster; and I was rightly wary of her. But there are two sides to a dragon. A dragon can be angry and fire-breathing, unpredictable and dangerous, attacking the village; but also lonely and forlorn, in his cave, with only his cold treasure for company, his own sad reflection in a thousand meaningless, shiny things. Every child knows that a dragon deserves pity.

I was tired, and my thoughts were slippery.

"I'm here, Mum," I said. "They've moved you to a new room. A private room, on your own." My breathing seemed short, perhaps from carrying the chair. "They're going to give you a painkiller." I couldn't say morphine because it sounded sinister in the circumstances, a drug that deadened pain but also hastened death. It sounded like a drug administered to subdue, and that reminded me of... but that was a time I didn't want to think about.

Warren started to influence my life before I even met him. My mother had never looked at the labels on food before, but now she read out" hydrogenated vegetable oil" and put the packet back on the supermarket shelf with the satisfaction of someone squashing a persistent fly. She pointed out the CCTV cameras going up in town and told me that although the satellites in the sky were too high for me to see, they could watch me when I bent to tie a shoelace. She hadn't started going out with Warren at that time, but she had met him through Paul, and it seemed that a whole group of them were going back to Warren's flat and talking through the night about the state of the world. "He's a brilliant man," my mother said. "He can see through all this -" and she made a broad-fingered gesture that encompassed food additives, multinational companies, media propaganda, arms dealers, fossil fuels, fluoride in water and carcinogenic mobile phones.

She was staying out later at night, and sleeping in, so I would make my own cup of tea before school, in the grubby kitchen at Cross Street. Darren had taped up a handwritten sign - 'Will everyone PLEASE wash up EVERYTHING before going to bed ' - but the sign had been splashed and smeared and the paper had wrinkled. Lisa was sometimes around in the mornings but she was quiet with me, and I suspected that she knew about my mother and Paul, even though my mother gleefully insisted that Lisa was a simpleton and suspected nothing. A divorced man called Peter had moved into the house and he was there at breakfast time, always smiling, stirring instant coffee and aiming the spoon at the sink like a dart before throwing it in with a clatter, eating his toast standing up and digging a buttery knife into his jam jar. "Another day at the grindstone, eh?" he grinned, as I put on my school shoes. My mother wasn't working at the time; she said she didn't want to be a "wage slave" any more. "I loved school," Peter went on, clapping his toast crumbs in the approximate direction of the sink. "Best days of your life, eh?"

I was in high school by this time, and my best friend was Sally Betteridge. She drew pictures of ponies. We sat together in most lessons, at a table halfway back, next to the soporific radiator. We used to dot our 'i's with big circles and sometimes, if the work was particularly boring, with hearts. We liked drawing the accents over letters in French, especially the circumflexes. I liked French and thought it was often more sensible than English: in English someone says 'it was a beautiful… 'and the next word could be hat, dog, or lasagne, so the word 'beautiful 'hangs meaninglessly, waiting to justify itself, while in French the adjective comes after the noun, as it does in your head: 'it was a garden beautiful. 'I tried to explain this to Sally but she just wrinkled her nose and said, "French is stupid."

I went to Sally's house for tea. Her family ate properly at the kitchen table, with cutlery laid out and ketchup in the middle, but

I couldn't eat because of the snotty little brothers and the smell of cat food by the back door. The fish fingers were brown inside. Sally's mum leaned close to me as she distributed the plates and said," I'm so glad Sally has finally made a friend." Sally's bedroom walls were papered with shiny pictures of ponies cut raggedly out of magazines.

I couldn't invite Sally back to mine. I pretended we lived in a very small flat, just as a stopgap before we moved into a new house. There were rumours at school about where I lived, and some of the nastier girls would make comments in the dinner queue.

My mum stayed out later and later, then one day she said Warren wanted to meet me. I was as nervous as if I were taking an exam, but when I got there Warren didn't really speak to me at all, or even look at me. My mum took me with her to his flat a few times after that; we stayed so late one night that I fell asleep in a chair, and felt sick when she woke me up and I had to crawl into the back of someone's car for a lift home. Warren's flat was thick with old chairs and piled cushions so all his friends could stuff themselves in, and there was heavy fabric stapled across the window instead of curtains, and brown-ringed coffee cups knocked over in awkward places. It was always dark, and he had an old-fashioned gas fire with only the central section lit, the tiny blue flames trickling across the yellow-brown ceramic grille. There would usually be two or three people there when we arrived, and more might come later; sometimes he had friends staying, with dreadlocks and sleeping bags, and I avoided using the bathroom because I wasn't sure who would be in there or what they would be doing.

Warren and his friends were talking about 9/11, but not in the way that everyone else talked about it. Everyone else talked about shock and tragedy, and used the word "awful" a lot; for me, the image that had stuck was a newspaper photo of a small dark figure falling in front of a skyscraper, someone who had jumped, pinned by the camera between life and death. Warren and his friends talked instead about the CIA, the FBI, the Saudis and Bush, and did lots of nodding and head shaking and told each other emphatically that the whole event was planned, funded, set up and covered up. When they talked about any subject they seemed to be taking turns to outdo each other, to press a story further and further; it was like a game of conversational pass-the-parcel, as each participant took hold of the subject from the previous speaker and ripped off another layer with a flourish, to reveal a deeper truth beneath.

I remember the rhythms of their conversations better than the actual subject matter. Sometimes everyone tried to speak at once, in a great surge of noise and gesture, but one voice would get through first and charge on while the others fell back, the dominant voice speaking rapidly and with absolute certainty while the listeners twitched and muttered restlessly; and then there would rise another swell of voices, another rush to be the first to surface. Sometimes little eddies of localised conversation would wash around the room, until someone with a strong voice and an unequivocal point to make picked everyone up again. As well as speech there were waved hands and exclamations, sarcastic laughs and faces pulled to extremes: sneers, frowns, extravagantly peaked eyebrows and twisted mouths.

The first time the subject of New Gaia came up it was mildly derided. "They're a bunch of hippies, aren't they?" someone said, and there was talk of idealists and realists and hypocrites, anarchists and syndicalists, and posh people playing at being poor. I came to realise, though, over time, that the ground was always gently shifting at Warren's, as if it were made of sand rather than earth: just as his friends drifted in and out of favour, his vigorous, definite opinions drifted too. Talk and people washed in and out, until New Gaia had become a plan, my mum was Warren's girlfriend, and we were all going to move there.

"Chicken shit," I said, and Mark laughed.

We were sitting on the bench outside Acorn Ward, and I had told him about the fire at Lucas Street, and he had put his arm around me, and then he asked me about what it was like when we lived at New Gaia.

"We didn't have any electricity the first year we were there," I told him, "and it was freezing. It was all candles and cold water and there was literally chicken shit everywhere."

Mark was smiling. "The mind boggles," he said. We were still waiting outside Acorn Ward, in the tiny garden, waiting to see my mum. Apparently she was still Being Assessed. Two more people came to the doorway to smoke; they didn't look particularly mad, and they were allowed to use a lighter. It was a disposable one, which they passed between them, made of clear green plastic so bright it looked like an enormous prismatic emerald.

"It wasn't so bad," I added, and we sat smiling for a while.

"They're taking a long time to assess her," Mark said eventually, still smiling, and shifting on the bench as if his back was stiff. "I hope she's not giving them too much trouble."

"It is her middle name," I said, making him laugh.

"Maybe, when we do get to see her, we should take her down to the hospital café or something. I imagine she'll want to get out of here."

"Will they let her leave the ward?"

"Maybe. She's not on the secure ward. She's not actually locked up, you know." I had assumed that the whole place was locked, the whole sinister psychiatric wing. Even this little square of garden, with its stunted bushes and smoking benches, was enclosed on all sides by walls.

"The secure ward is there." Mark pointed to the windows on our right, and I looked in, but as far as I could see the room inside looked like the sitting room of a cheap guest house, with higgledy chairs and a TV." That's Chestnut Ward. Your mum's on Acorn Ward." Then he grinned and lowered his voice. "Do you think all the wards are named after nuts?"

On one of our last nights at Cross Street I woke up in the dark and my mother wasn't there. I knew, rationally, that she was just staying late at Warren's, but I felt a panic in the room as if she had been abducted or run away. I had fallen out of the habit of sleeping alone. I lay looking at her empty bed and it felt like a tooth that had been pulled. It struck me that the absence of a person can be bigger than their presence: when they're missing, all the space and silence that they used to occupy as they moved and spoke and listened is emptied, but vibrating with what might have been. I couldn't have lived without her. I lay for a long time looking at her empty bed, but I fell asleep before she came back.

We had only a month's notice to give on our room, and the landlord's agent, a trim girl in a grey skirt, started bringing prospective tenants to look over the place while we were still there. They trailed after her through the communal rooms, but in our room she stepped to the side and unleashed them to examine our windows, ceiling and floor. They crowded into the room and poked around, staring at our stuff. They sat heavily on our beds and asked questions about the carpet and curtains. They didn't look at me; I was no longer part of this room.

One young woman said," Would I be allowed to paint the walls? I couldn't live with this colour." I was sitting cross-legged on my bed, pretending to do my homework, pretending the intruders weren't there. Even though I hadn't chosen the colour of the walls, I was offended that my home had been insulted.

Later, there was a gentle knock on the door of our room, and when I opened it, puzzled because no-one ever knocked on the door of our room, and half-expecting to open up a magical reality as children do in books, it was Lisa. She came in. I had tidied up the room before the arrival of the landlord's agent, so all my underwear and dirty washing was stuffed away, but, far more embarrassingly, I was playing with my Polly Pocket set, the plastic case wide open on the bed to reveal the dolls in their little house. They had been packing for the move, although for them their house went with them and moving meant the imminent arrival of a tornado that would carry them away to a strange and possibly frightening land. I had decided that one doll, Peggy, was nervous, and she wanted to tie herself into the wardrobe in case the move was too violent; but the confident doll, Alice, was reassuring, and even excited, wondering where they would be when they next opened their front door. I had lost myself in their conversation when Lisa came in and I felt myself blushing hotly, as if I had been caught speaking aloud their tiny voices. Lisa, though, didn't look at them; her eyes were thoroughly exploring the rest of the room.

I explained that my mother wasn't in.

"She's not in much at all, these days, is she?" said Lisa. "Anyway, I didn't come to see her, I came to see you. I wanted to give you a goodbye present. Just a little thing, just to say goodbye."

She handed me a small carrier bag without actually looking at me, since her eyes were drawn to the miscellaneous heaps of possessions on top of the chest of drawers. I put my hand in the bag and pulled out a silvery bangle in the shape of a snake, the head coiled around the tip of the tail to make a complete loop. I thanked her and pushed it over the thick part of my hand on to my wrist. Lisa was still looking around the room; momentarily she would force her eyes to return to me, but they were impatient to scramble away, searching the room like sniffer dogs.

"Anyway," she said, "you can show that to your mum, can't you? When she comes back." We hugged impassively, and said goodbye, and then she left, turning stiffly to give her eyes one last sweep of the room.

The morphine was administered by a machine, like a fat bicycle pump with a motor, resting on her bed alongside her. It hummed quietly, warm with confident technology. A single tube looped under her sheet and I couldn't see where the morphine entered her. There were no other wires or tubes or monitors in this room; they had all been left behind.

She didn't look or sound any different but I could now believe she was in a dream, not a nightmare, contentedly intoxicated by a painkilling drug, and I had done my duty as next-of-kin and ensured she was made comfortable.

I sat with her without speaking, without touching her. I had left the door ajar, because with the door closed the private room was almost too private, here in the centre of a busy hospital building but shut up like a secret. With the door open I could hear the evening patter and murmur of the nurses and an occasional distant crisis. A conversation walked past - "no, that was last week when" - and later a squeaky wheel was brought steadily down the corridor and manoeuvred awkwardly through a door.

She was still breathing, her lungs as calm and mechanical as the morphine machine. It felt like she could go on forever in this muted state.

Nothing happened, and when it got late I went home.

I was tired, so I just ate toast and went to bed. I felt disconnected from my normal life, as if I was at a retreat or a boot camp, and my usual routines had been suspended. My sitting room was unsat in and my kitchen was cold. Perhaps I was already in a period of mourning.

With the light off it was very dark in my bedroom, the monochrome shapes impossible to identify without the map in my head. I had long become accustomed to the safety of sleeping alone, and here, in the dark, in my bed, in my bedroom, in my house, I was in a box in a box in a box, the smallest and cosiest Russian doll.

Only then, when I was hidden in bed, could I bring out the thoughts that had come to me earlier and look at them. The administration of morphine had reminded me of another time, many years ago, when she was "given something to calm her down" - chemically subdued - with my consent. I hadn't visited her then. She was in Chestnut Ward then, the secure ward. When they said they were giving her something to calm her down I had pictured her as a lion, crawling and snarling and dribbling, with a tranquilliser dart hanging from its flank. It was frightening how on two occasions now, powerful drugs had been given to her at my instigation. I had only to say yes and she was helplessly injected. I saw myself as a Roman Emperor with my thumb turned down - or no, I was more like an anonymous informant, sneaking out of a phone booth.

As I swam towards sleep I imagined myself behind the magistrates bench, sentencing her, the courtroom reversed and strange." What the hell are you doing?" she snarled at me, as the security officers 'keys rattled in the lock of the door behind her.

Wednesday

"No, no, we're *absolutely fine* without you," Alison said. "There's no need to think about rushing back to work." Her voice became indistinct, as if a box had fallen over her head, and after a moment's confusion I realised she was speaking to someone else. I could picture her, pressing the receiver into her shoulder, twisting round to call out a question, or jab at a keyboard, or dig deeply into mess of pointlessly printed-out paperwork. "You take as long as you need," she added, coming back to me briefly, as if leaning in through a door on her way past. "Actually Sharon's come in today - you know, she's desperate for the hours - she says she can work the rest of the week, so don't you worry at all."

Sharon works part time, but she's been scrounging for more hours since her husband retired. She jokes about him being under her feet, driving her mad; she shakes her head, deadpan: "Honestly," she says, "I might have to break out the rat poison." Someone else told me that she needs the hours because they're desperate for money, pensions being worth nothing these days. Sharon is loud, a personality, bustling about the corridors with aggressive bonhomie. I could picture her running my courtroom, snatching importantly at her gown as her busy rushing left it floating behind, coming up to the bench between cases with her quips, making the court clerk laugh. I felt a dull jealousy.

I was sitting in my mother's room at the hospital, listening to the mid-morning activity in the corridor outside, a flow of footsteps and trolleys and mumbled exchanges. The small room I sat in was very quiet and still. The walls in here were the colour of milk, smooth and wipe-clean, except for a strip of rubbery grey plastic that cut through the whole hospital at trolley-height to protect against bumps. The linoleum floor had a discreet pattern of swirls, which each contained tinier swirls, each composed of still tinier

77

grains in an endless microscopic fractal. The linoleum curved upwards when it met the walls and continued vertically for a few inches, so that the floor was actually a sort of shallow bowl, a scoop for containing liquid mess. We were all walking around with our feet in a scrubbed tray, sticky with disinfectant.

The window was a bright white square. It showed nothing, but persistently summoned my eyes, so it could print in them a large dark square that showed everywhere I looked. Alison at work would have called it "a headache on a plate"; she said that about shafts of sunlight, overly warm rooms or long sessions in front of the computer. "That's a headache on a plate, that is," she'd say, squinting.

The only fixture in the blank room was the sink attached to the wall, which should have reminded me of the washbasin in our room at Willow House; but the pink washbasin at Willow House was homely and grubby and close friends with the old chest, the rumpled bed, the fretful wallpaper and the noisily patterned carpet, whereas this was an efficient, severe sink sticking out of a bare wall into a bare room, a white, modern sink, small and square, with huge chrome elbow taps overhanging it gracelessly. It reminded me more of the toilets in the cells at the magistrates court: the only fittings in each cell are a screwed-down bench and a toilet that doesn't look like a toilet, just a metal funnel fixed to the wall.

There was a small mirror above this sink, actually a mirrored tile, included among the neat rectangle of white tiles, but I could only see the wall reflected in it. I didn't want to see myself or my mother; it was bad enough being here without having to witness myself being here. Above the mirror there was a short shelf, bearing disposable medical items: a box of tissues or wipes and a box of something else, perhaps plastic gloves. They were part of the work world of the staff, everyday brands to them, delivered in huge boxes of sixty or a hundred and distributed by an unseen man in overalls. The shelf was held in place by two brackets, one unsymmetrically closer to the edge than the other; for a long time this bothered me, and my eyes kept returning to wonder why the brackets weren't even, until I eventually saw a hairline crack in a tile that must have frightened off the drill and necessitated the second bracket being placed further along than originally intended.

The bed was not a fitting or fixture in the room but a disposable addition; or rather an interchangeable addition, like a car in a garage or a bag in a locker. The hospital bed was a high, clumsy piece of equipment, constructed of steel tubes coated generously with plastic the colour of cheap chocolate milkshake. There were castor wheels with a chunky footbrake on each, and multiple bars at the ends and sides, some of which unhooked and hinged down or up to make the bed less or more like a baby's cot. I had seen the nurses operate the bed expertly, like workmen using a crane or a drill, clipping and switching and adjusting, reaching here and kicking there, circling it methodically and intently.

From where I sat I could see the sturdy little wheels, all turned at independent angles but clamped still by their heavy rubber brakes. Above, the tubular cage had been folded down, and a white sheet drifted out over the side. And in the bed, she was still there, her chest steadily rising and falling as her lungs and throat and nose moved air in and out with a coarse, glutinous noise.

New Gaia wasn't a hippy commune. It was a big dilapidated house, in overgrown grounds, owned by a couple in their sixties called Bernard and Layla. Bernard was grey and whiskery like an old English sheepdog, and Layla was tangerine-haired and flustered. The house was too ramshackle to sell, and they didn't have money to fix it, so they had invited artists and musicians, and then environmentalists, self-sufficiency seekers and anarchists, to create a kind of catch-all retreat. From time to time these people, who sometimes blended perfectly, would suddenly crunch up against their differences, the artists eating mass-produced, meaty junk food and the environmentalists lecturing them, and Layla would start screaming at everyone until a consensus was reached that she was the only thorn in the harmonious garden.

It sometimes seemed that it wasn't the inhabitants that were going back to nature, but rather the house itself. Ivy was able to grow right through the walls, between the bricks and the window frames, and various moulds spread vigorously, new colonies striking out in every room. A whole buddleia, practically a tree, was growing out of the side of the chimney, heavy with ripe purple flowers. Until then, I had always believed in the simple equation that big houses were worth a lot of money, but Bernard explained gloomily that big houses are only worth a lot of money if you have a lot of money to spend on them. New Gaia was a liability, not an asset. Owning it was like having a big family to raise, a dozen children needing feeding and clothing; as soon as one was satisfied, there was another one crying out for shoes. The beams in the roof had "dropped", the damp course was "shot through" and there was "likely as not wet rot" under the floors; Bernard degenerated into asthmatic muttering whenever he tried to explain all that needed doing, or had not been done, or would most likely never be done.

The layout of the house was as random as if it had been put together in a dream. Downstairs melted into upstairs, as there were rooms off a landing halfway up; there were bedrooms downstairs and rooms upstairs too rotten to sleep in. There was a big empty room with a big damp wall, almost black, and just a hole for a fireplace, with bird droppings in the hearth. There were rooms with wallpaper half ripped off, leaving great crests of white like the tops of waves. There were beautiful stained glass panes around the front door, and a geometric mosaic of cool terracotta tiles on the floor in the hall. The first day we arrived, Joseph's dog came skittering across the tiles to slobber at us, and Bernard conducted us through into the kitchen. "Come in, come in," he kept saying, even when we were already in." Come in, come in! Mitzi will be so pleased to see you; Mitzi loves new people." He fussed about us and our bags and bundles while the dog licked something on the floor. "I'll give Mitzi a call - I don't know why she's not here - I know she wanted to be here when you arrived - Mitzi! Darling! I'll go and find her - " and we were left alone in the kitchen, greeted by no-one else in this house supposedly founded on the notion of community.

There were other people living there, of course, and people who moved in after us, and people who moved out. There was a sculptor called Tori and an artist called Joseph, both of whom had hollowed out studios for themselves in the various cluttered outbuildings, like hedgehogs making nests in woodpiles. There was an enthusiastic vegetable grower called Andy, and an odd chap called Frank who fell out with Layla and left soon after we arrived. There was a tenaciously bad-tempered friend of Warren's called Steven, or Moody Steve, as my mother took to calling him; and then there was Warren, my mum, me, and Paul, newly arrived and elbowing in.

There was no electricity when we first lived there. Warren and Steve were both excited at being "off grid", beholden to no-one, dependent on our own resources. Water came from a well and went into a cesspit; Warren and Steve took it all as proof that a person could "live off the land," but Bernard pointed out mildly that the water supply was filtered and inspected annually by a multinational chemical company, and the cesspit was emptied at shocking expense by an enormous stinking lorry that ripped half the hedge off when it backed up, beeping, down the drive.

There was an Aga in the kitchen, but it stood cold because someone had argued passionately that refined oil was evil. There was a capacious ceramic sink with two taps - tall, old-fashioned taps on sticks - but both ran cold; or rather, vomited splats of cold water in distressed gulps when you twisted their stiff, star-shaped handles. The pipes convulsed and moaned, and when the taps were painfully screwed shut there was an abrupt shudder and then silence, as if a heavy door had been slammed on a wailing prisoner. Food was cooked on a woodburning stove, black with soot, and the whole house smelled of smoke. The handle had broken on the firebox door, so someone had to use an old poker to unhook it so that wood could be chucked in; the fire would crackle and spark and shift irritably. Later, in the winter, we conceded to refined oil, and the Aga was permanently and gloriously lit, warm and hissing, and smelling of oil like an old steam locomotive. We even had the bliss of hot water then: it was a joy even to wash up, immersing my hands in the deep sink until they were bright red to the elbows.

Food was haphazard and contentious. There were days of communal cooking and resolute planning, days of bitter dispute and recrimination, and days of retreat and retrenchment, each man for himself. Vegetables were grown in the garden but they ripened in gluts: for a week or so we had to eat courgettes, another week small, black-hearted potatoes, another week lettuce left ragged by caterpillars. Andy kept tomato plants on the kitchen windowsill and the tiny tomatoes ripened one at a time. They tasted of stale water. Most of us bought food from a local farm shop, or a convenience store in the village; Warren and Joseph both had cars. My mum wouldn't cook on the woodburner, but Warren boiled us eggs or brown rice or tins of oxtail soup.

There were always eggs, because there were chickens, roaming the garden with their slow, deliberate strides, wading through the long grass. They were fancy chickens, with silky shuttlecock bodies, tight little neck feathers and stiff plumes at their tails, their dinosaur feet emerging from fat feathered pantaloons. They combed the grass flat clawing for worms, and they left everywhere their droppings: soft brown smears, speckled and crusted with white, stuck to the coarse blades of grass, smeared to sludge across the path, often walked into the kitchen. I always wore shoes in the house.

We had a chicken feeder, a round tin like a lampshade that let the feed shake down into a tray. It had to be kept well away from the house, though, because it attracted rats. Layla turned white and then pink at the mention of rats, and Warren and Andy enjoyed the grim project of trying out different traps. I saw a dead rat once, long and grey, with tiny curled-up paws and yellow teeth that jutted uncomfortably out of its mouth. Sometimes at night there were scurrying noises, and Warren put on his trousers and stalked the house bare-chested with a shovel.

The garden was enormous; when you reached a hedge there was always another part of the garden on the other side, flowing into crumbling outbuildings, twisted trees and a choked pond. There was even a full-height polytunnel - white plastic sheeting stretched over a frame of hoops, like a large plastic greenhouse - where Bernard had once grown cannabis. The metal skeleton had rusted and the plastic was torn and flapping in places; inside, the plants had turned yellow and stringy. There was no electricity for the lamps and pumps, and the whole life support system stood dead, like obsolete technology. Dry weeds and nettles had come up beneath the wooden benches, fed by condensation or leaks from the blustery plastic roof.

Bernard had a chair in the polytunnel, a white plastic garden chair with a cushion on the seat, and a small coffee table with carved legs, stuck with dead snail shells, upon which he placed his mug of tea, cigarette papers, and tobacco. There was no chair for anyone else, but he was friendly if I stood in the doorway. "Just the pickings," he said, "just the last leftovers," and he carefully rolled himself a thin cigarette and foraged for a bit of dead leaf from amongst his plants like a gorilla picking a flea from its mate. "I meant to grow tulips in here at one time," he'd say, or "Bit of a wind up today, isn't there?" Bernard had a beard that grew up his face like grass spreading across a forgotten path; the odd whisker even sprouted on his cheekbones. "Mitzi loves tulips," he'd say. "We were in Amsterdam in the sixties..."

It took a while for me to realise that Mitzi was Bernard's pet name for Layla, and I never shook off the feeling that there really was another person in the house, called Mitzi. Bernard spoke of Mitzi as a charming, gentle person - "Mitzi found a newt in that pond one year," he said fondly - and I imagined her as a ghostly extra person, floating somewhere in the house. Bernard lit his roll-up with a match, the cigarette as tiny as a matchstick itself in his big face, and he reached for his tea - "Look at that," he'd say, "I've let it go cold again." He wore sandals, and his toes were hairy. "I used to have three sugars," he said, "but Mitzi got me down to one."

At the top of the house there was a strange attic. Part of it had been turned into a proper room, with wallpaper and a sloping ceiling, but a gap in the internal wall, a doorway without a door, let into the untamed part of the attic, a dark and dusty framework of wood, like the hold of an ancient, creaking ship. There was nowhere to put your feet, but if you stayed long enough to let your eyes adjust you could see the underside of the roof tiles, overlapping behind thin beams of coarse unsanded wood, almost like a woven pattern. Looking into this attic space was like seeing the truth behind a facade: you could see how a roof was stuck together. The room that had been built at one end of the attic felt to me like a little shelter constructed hopefully in a wild wood, feeble against the forces of storms and monsters.

It was Warren's idea that I would love to sleep in the attic room. "What an adventure!" he said. "I'd have loved this when I was a kid." His big shape in the small room had the look of an oversized action figure in a dolls 'house. He had to bend his neck against the slope of the ceiling. "Any kid would love this," he said.

Paul had initially slept in the attic room, but he had migrated into the library, setting up camp in there one day without comment or explanation. The library was a downstairs room, properly furnished, with full-height shelves of books untouched for years, sagging armchairs that looked like old men too tired to get up, and a fusty smell like vinegar mixed with mildew. No-one used the room and Paul had literally made camp in a corner, a bivouac of khaki sleeping bag and rucksack with a camouflage net slung from the backs of chairs to give him privacy. I almost expected him to light a campfire in the mouth of his den, on the threadbare carpet. The room Bernard had allocated to Warren, Mum and me was the small bedroom off the half-landing." I'm afraid it's not a big room," he said, again and again." I suppose you might charitably call it cosy." There was a single bed, so Warren took the legs off the divan and laid it flat on the floor with the mattress beside it, to make a big double, with a duvet to sleep on and a duvet to sleep underneath, so that he and Mum had a big, comfortable nest that filled the room. He talked about painting a giant mural on the wall when he could get hold of some paints.

Someone found me a camp bed, and straightened it, unfolding it with rusty jolts until the cricks were cracked and it stood steady. "There, that's just fine," everyone murmured in approval, but Warren said it didn't fit in the bedroom, and after a week or so he took it up to the attic for me. He couldn't figure out how to fold it properly, so it looked like a big insect with broken legs and wings when he carried it up. Warren bought me a sleeping bag, a mummy bag, he called it, like the shroud of an entombed Egyptian mummy. He presented it to me like it was a special present. It was a sleeping bag with a hood, and I could wriggle down into it and pull a drawstring at my chin so that only my face was showing. The camp bed was like an old-fashioned sun lounger: a taut canvas hammock strung inside a metal frame on long squeaking springs. Inside the sleeping bag, suspended from the frame on the hammock, I felt like a grub in a cocoon, bound in silk and hanging from a twig, helpless. If I panicked in the night, I knew there was no rapid escape: I would have to squirm out of the sleeping bag, crawl out of the camp bed without flipping it, and then find with my feet the top of the wooden stepladder without falling; and if I did make it down onto the landing below, where would I run to? I could only sit on the steps outside Mum and Warren's room, in the dark, on my own. So I buried deep inside my sleeping bag, pretending it was armoured or protected by sorcery, and on hot nights my sweat would seep into it and leave me breathless and slippery by morning.

In the autumn, before the Aga was allowed, the house grew cold. The days were shortening and the sun fading, and wind and rain tore at the bedraggled garden and goaded the house. We were all drawn to the kitchen and the heat of the woodburner. There was a long farmhouse table, deeply grooved and sticky, and a number of mismatched chairs, all of which wobbled or caught their spindly legs clumsily against the fat legs of the table. As the woodburner smoked and sputtered, occasionally making us jump with a crack of wood as sharp as gunfire, we huddled, bored, in jumpers and gloves, with mugs of black tea, as the room grew dark. Sometimes there was bickering, or palpable silent irritation; Joseph and Warren might be picking at each other, or Bernard trying to soothe Layla, or Warren and my mother sniggering about someone and pulling faces across the table. Everyone went to bed early.

I had, however, a new and unexpected gift of privacy: my daily trip to school. To get to the high school from New Gaia I had to catch a slow, meandering bus to the town where we used to live, and then a jolting, frenetic bus full of kids from the town centre to the school, through the rush hour traffic. I caught the rural bus at ten past seven, and the solitude of early morning was bliss, even in the rain; the bus lumbered unhurriedly along the narrow lanes and turned into still narrower lanes, sometimes even deviating from due south to due north, to call upon every tiny village or hamlet, edging between cottages like a big friendly giant attending a children's tea party. The villages were asleep except for the few familiar but quietly anonymous faces that took the same bus as me every day. The journey was long and slow, and I gave myself over to it, enjoying the undisturbed time to daydream and the steady motion, which gave me a feeling of gently charging up, like a muted dynamo.

I even enjoyed the uncomfortable, coarse seat: it was like a private cubicle, and at the stops I could rest my head against the cold, moist glass and look out at the closed curtains of people still asleep. No-one looked at me or spoke to me. Mark once told me that therapists suggest you identify a "special place", a place you've known where you felt safe and happy, where you can imagine yourself to be when you need to escape the present. I thought at once of that bus ride to school, my perfect special place, a place where I was always moving forward but contentedly at rest.

I went to the hospital cafeteria too early for lunch, and they were only serving toasted teacakes. There were salads of pasta or couscous in plastic tubs lined up in the chiller, so I chose a tub of cold pasta in tomato sauce, dotted with miniature balls of mozzarella that looked like plastercine.

In hindsight, my life at New Gaia seemed exciting, like one of those disasters in life that turn into a good story. It was easier to enjoy when it was no longer happening. Perhaps we should cope with all life's difficult chapters by projecting them into a future past. These days in the hospital will become a memory; I will tell my friend Emma about the brain scan and the move to a single room and the morphine. I can choose to tell the story so as to make her sympathetic; or shocked; or I could even choose to make her laugh at the absurdity of tragedy. I will tell the story of these days to people I haven't even met yet; the story of how my mother died.

I was already regretting the pasta salad. At the counter they were setting out the hot food and there were smells of cauliflower cheese and chicken curry. I had chosen poorly and spoilt my lunch.

At the table next to mine an older man in glasses was just finishing a toasted teacake, holding the last piece gingerly to keep his thumb out of the glistening butter. He had badly combed grey hair and a heightened, slightly startled manner. He licked his fingers and snatched at a paper napkin to dry them. Then he spotted me looking at him. His eyes were quick and anxious and pounced on me before I could react and look away; he smiled, so I smiled back.

"You visiting someone?" he asked.

I nodded. "My mum."

"I'm visiting my wife, Elena," he said. He kept rummaging in the paper napkin with his fingers, as if he couldn't get them clean, and he shifted his legs as he talked, as if he couldn't rest. "She's been in five days already - Lord knows when she'll be out, they say they need to do more tests." He discarded the paper napkin but almost at once picked it back up again. "She's got angina, they think; I mean, she's always been a bit overweight, not that fit, but she's been awfully breathless lately. She said to me, she said, I'm not as young as I used to be, but I said well I'm not either but I can still get up the stairs in one go!" He chuckled and then stopped abruptly. "She has to stop halfway up, leaning on the rail, not right really. She had to see the doctor, and he referred her up here, we got a quick appointment, they were very good, I just wish they didn't have to keep her in, it seemed like they were all of a panic... who did you say, your mother is it?"

"Yes," I said. "She's had a stroke. She's in a bad way." I felt self-consciously grown up, like a child using adults 'language.

"Oh, that's dreadful," he said. "Still, we all get old, don't we? It comes to us all."

"It does," I said.

"You've just got to get on and enjoy life, haven't you?" he said.

"You have," I said.

"I mean, any of us could get knocked down by a bus, couldn't we? You've got to enjoy it while you can, haven't you?"

I noticed that his eyes were suddenly shiny, so I nodded and looked down at my pasta salad. My mother used to say that life was there to be lived, but she meant that you had to fight it, shake it to get the enjoyment out. She abhorred contentment. I remembered an argument she had once with Mark. "You have to push yourself forward more," she was saying, insistently. They must have been talking about his work. "It's a dog eat dog world."

"I don't see it that way," Mark replied mildly, and I could feel my mother's anger swelling, like the anger of a boy racer stuck behind a caravan. "You're such a fucking idiot!" she snapped. For her, the good things in life could only come at someone else's expense. They had to be fought for and won.

"I think she'll be alright," the man at the next table said. He was talking about his wife again. "She's always been very strong. Always kept me in line!" He laughed, leaning towards me and showing teeth flecked with silver-grey fillings. I smiled back at him.

"We've been married thirty-nine years," he said, proudly.

"Gosh!" I exclaimed.

My mother used to pursue Mark around the house when she was in the mood for conflict, her face feverish. "Don't walk away from me!" she would yell.

"I don't want to argue," he would say, moving sideways, face tilted, out of the door.

"Don't walk away from me!"

"There's no point in this." He would hold the door like a shield. "We'll talk properly when we've calmed down."

"Don't fucking walk away, you fucking fucker!" He would be trudging upstairs with his head bowed and his hands up, like a prisoner, and she would be screaming, flecks of spit following him up the stairs. Although he was moving, it seemed as if he was the one who was immovable, solid and still, while she, at the foot of the stairs, vibrated with violence and frenzy.

Warren used to fight with her. There were rows in the night and rows in the day, snatches of abuse as doors were flung open or slammed. Once at New Gaia she threw his clothes out of the window and he had to go down to fetch them, with a sheet wrapped round him like a toga, naked underneath. There was a coffee stain on their bedroom wall where a mug had smashed: an exploded splat from which long vertical streams had dribbled down to the floor, like a piece of modern art. The rhythm of their rows was discordant, experimental music: there would be a shout, a slam, a mumble, a silence; then two voices shouting at once in a tumbling cacophony, a dreadful pause, then a clear, bitter voice enunciating clear, foul words; then rising, interrupting, crying, stamping; another silence, then a wail like a gunshot. There was a sense that anything could happen next, that glass might smash or blood might spill. The whole house was tense and flinching.

Once Warren poured beer over her head. She rushed after him to throw a shoe; she looked oddly small and sticky, flat-haired and big-eyed like an animal. Another time she snapped Warren's sunglasses and they looked strange and comical, each piece a single lens with a useless dangling arm. Their fights trailed destruction, a wake of random broken things. My mother, though, was satisfied, as if a payment had been exacted. Later, when she was calm, she would say," Oh, it's only a cup," as if the fight had a value beyond material things.

"Anyway." The man at the next table stood up, his fingers still worrying the crumpled paper napkin. "I must get back to my wife. I hope your, ah, mother gets better soon."

I smiled and nodded, and watched him trundle away, held up briefly by a woman with an unwieldy pushchair. I didn't finish my pasta salad.

Back in the room, my mother hadn't changed. We sat again in silence. Outside in the corridor I could hear the sound of visiting time, and I felt that maybe I ought to say something, to offer a contribution in some way.

"I had a pasta salad," I said. "In one of those plastic tubs, a prepared one. It was horrible: there were mozzarella balls that were like bits of rubber."

My voice dropped like a stone into the silent room. I stopped speaking, and it was more difficult to start again. It seemed inappropriate, too, to be telling a dying person about a disappointing lunch. I ought to have something real to say, something important, but I couldn't think of anything. Perhaps life is just trivia: food, silly jokes, shopping. What else is there? Getting caught in the rain makes us miserable, a cup of tea comforts us. Even a condemned man is consoled by an extra-special last meal.

"I don't really know what to say," I said suddenly, out loud. This time the words didn't drop, but burned brightly in the middle of the room. They hung there, charged with portent and significance, like poetry, but I had nothing to say to them either. Did I mean something simple or profound?

The silence slowly rolled back in.

At New Gaia there was a potter called Tori. She had her workshop in an old outbuilding, part stone and part wood, and everything inside, including Tori herself, was a warm grey from the aura of clay, dark and wet or dry and dusty. There were shelves fitted with racks for drying pots, like racks of buns in a bakery, and bottles of chemicals for glazes and paints, and a huge bag of clay sagging like an old dog in a corner. Tori sat at a heavy wheel, which spun steadily as she worked the foot pedal, slowly and firmly, like a person cycling up a very gentle hill. She wore big check shirts and dirty, baggy jeans, but she was slight, not mannish, with blond hair that she knotted loosely at the back of her head with a brown band. When it started to slip she absently pulled the band onto her wrist, gathered up her hair, and expertly slid the band from her wrist over the bundle of hair, snapping it tight. All her movements were sure and unselfconscious.

Her hands were crusted with whitening clay, and sometimes she sat picking it out of her nails as we talked. When she threw a pot on the wheel she dipped her hands in water and their coating of clay became dark, like very wet brown icing, as the pot skimmed past her slow fingers and magically changed shape.

She told me that Tori was short for Victoria, but it seemed to me that Victoria would be a completely different person. In her workshop I sat on a wooden stool. "A three legged stool never wobbles, even if the floor is uneven," she told me, smiling. I tried to wobble my stool, but it felt almost glued to the concrete floor. She let me play about with pieces of clay; sometimes a wet squidgy piece, sometimes a firm, unworked, unfriendly piece. "It's all about patience," she said, starting up the wheel again.

I had rows with my mum. We argued about nothing; afterwards, I couldn't remember how it had started but I felt angry and wronged. "It's one of life's ironies," Tori said, "that the people we love most are the people we get the most angry with." She had her paints out, a palette dashed with red and orange, and she was pinching a tiny brush to a vase as it turned on the wheel, leaving a

90

perfect fine line of red around its circumference. "Of course, it makes sense: it's because you care about someone that you get so worked up about them."

She had built herself a brick kiln, away from the house, at the edge of the patch of weed-crazed paving where cars were parked. When she was firing she stoked it with wood for hours, tending it with intensive care, and I could smell the smoke from my attic room. Sometimes there were pots that hadn't fired properly, and she showed me patches that were burnt or crumbled. "It's like baking," she said. "You never know if the cake is going to rise."

When the evenings grew darker, she worked by oil lamp, and her workshop was dowsed in the lamp's rich smell and yellow light. Against the cold she wore gloves, a scarf and a woollen hat that folded down over her ears. Even later, when the house had electricity, there was none in the outbuildings. If, after school, I visited Tori, I sat on my stool talking to her until it was dark and then stepped out into the black garden with the light of the oil lamp wavering behind me like a magical spirit, and through the shapes of the trees I could see the electric lights of the house glaring in the uncurtained windows, unwelcoming and stark.

In the winter, in the house, people accumulated in the kitchen, drawn to the radiating heat of the newly fuelled Aga. I sat at the chunky table to do my homework, carefully edging my books between smears of butter and glasses of wine. People appeared in odd combinations, behaving differently according to who they found themselves drawn with. If Steve was across the table from Paul he would be lecturing him on the carcinogenic properties of breakfast cereals or the Jewish conspiracy, gesturing with his fork and slapping the ketchup bottle; if he found himself in the kitchen with Layla while she brewed herbal tea he was quieter and gentler with his opinions and tone of voice, even equanimous, like a man politely holding a door open for a woman. Layla herself was jumpy around Steve, Warren or Joseph, her jaw and shoulders held stiffly and her hands fumbling self-consciously to slice bread or dig for a teaspoon; but if only Bernard, Andy or women were present she moved with a confident swish and drawled," Oh Bernard, darling, will you take out the rubbish?" in a tone of comfortable

91

exasperation. The different behaviours of the housemates in different company reminded me of those magazine articles explaining how to wear the same skirt in three different ways: smart for work, dressed up for evenings and dressed down for weekends. I suppose I, too, behaved differently in reflection to who was in the room, although mostly I sat silently, as silent as the table, wearing my homework as an invisibility cloak.

Warren and my mum spent most of the cold winter in bed. "When I was your age," Warren said, "I was always out with my mates. I had loads of friends and my parents never saw me. I was always up to something. I didn't hang around at home." I didn't have loads of friends. Sally had melted into a little group of girls who used hair straighteners and carried handbags; they talked about *Big Brother* and *Pop Idol*, neither of which I had seen. I had no access to television. Sally had soaked up the way the other girls spoke and dressed, ending her sentences with an upward inflection, sharing music on their iPods with one earbud each, and wearing huge hoop earrings while walking to school and then taking them out, whispering urgently and pulling big-eyed expressions, before the teachers saw them. The group of girls had absorbed Sally like a sponge, but to me they were shiny, hard people, and I seemed to slide right off the surface of them.

Before we had electricity in the house the worst thing was washing. Water had to be boiled in a heavy, archaic kettle on the woodburner and carried up to the bath. Two kettlefuls and a hefty blast of cold water provided a lukewarm bath about three inches deep. I had to roll and squirm to stay warm; it was like being hungry and having to pick up rice grain by grain. I stretched out my legs and brought them together to slosh the water from side to side, across my skin and off again, the moisture evaporating and raising goosebumps up my thighs. If I lay down on my back, knees up, it was impossible to sit up again without shivering.

To wash my hair, my mother poured water over me from a plastic beaker; whichever way I tilted my head the froth always ran in my face and I protested while she fumed. "Can't she do that for herself?" Warren said. There was no lock on the bathroom door. I often cried, crunching myself up, cold and naked in the puddle of water. "Oh, for fuck's sake!" Mum would shout. My eyes were scoured with shampoo and tears. "You baby her too much," said Warren, slouched on the doorframe.

Even when we had electricity it was difficult to wash: an immersion heater slowly warmed a small tank and someone was always waiting for it. Baths had to booked and haggled over. The water was hot but the air was freezing; my thighs glowed red and steam drifted up like dry ice. Winter was cold at New Gaia, a hollow, deadening cold that you couldn't escape from. Sometimes there was a voice in my head every few minutes saying "I'm cold", as if I should do something about it. At bedtime I climbed up to my attic as vigorously as I could, to top up my muscles with heat, and then quickly pulled on several layers of clothing, to keep the precious heat from dribbling away.

All through the winter, from October to May, there was a smell of damp in the house, but I only noticed it when I first walked in. It was as if the smell seeped into me, and I became part of the house. It set me wondering whether the smell seeped out of me when I arrived at school. Perhaps I smelled of the house, of damp and mildew and herbal tea and woodburner. School had a smell of its own: the smell of adolescence, of PE socks and afternoon underarms. Perhaps that smell, too, seeped into me while I was there. Perhaps I smelled of school when I arrived at New Gaia, and of New Gaia when I arrived at school, like someone perpetually wearing the wrong uniform.

In the afternoon the same two nurses came to wash my mother, and the large nurse greeted me like a friend. "And how are we today?" she cried, addressing my mother as she circled the bed, shaking out a plastic apron and tying it round her middle. "How are we doing? You grab the gloves there, Lena... How are we feeling today?" She kept moving as she spoke, taking hold of equipment deftly, and when she caught my eye she smiled. "We'll give Mum a wash now, change of nightie, a good clean up. Do you want to go and grab a coffee? We'll be about fifteen minutes."

I stood up, scraping my chair out of their way, and as I stood I caught a quick glimpse of myself in the mirror above the sink. I was shocked by my face. I had assumed I was looking callous and bored; but my expression wasn't either. I looked tired, and worried, and scared, even lost. Bewildered, frightened. Then my reflection disappeared as the nurses rumbled the curtain along its pole, and I went out into the corridor.

I went to the cafe again, and bought a slice of lemon meringue pie. The meringue was tall and fluffy, with soft toasted peaks, and the filling was a bright glossy yellow. When I ate it, though, it was just sweet and sticky, with no texture or flavour. There was nothing to chew on and I just moved it around in my mouth.

Warren said to me: "Where's your spirit? Where's your energy?" My mother pulled a face and looked away. We were in the warm kitchen; Joseph was shaking dry food out for his dog and there was a sharp stink from the dusty biscuits. "Kids these days are half dead," Warren went on. "It's the diet they've been on since birth."

I had my homework open in front of me but I wasn't seeing it. Bernard was across the table, filling in a form of some sort. He squinted and adjusted his glasses and didn't look up. He wrote in careful capital letters, pressing hard with a black biro.

"They feed kids cheap junk, chemicals, anything to keep them quiet," Warren went on. "Artificial food for the mass production of obedient drones. It doesn't matter if it gives us all cancer once we're past childbearing age, even better if it kills us off before we get old and useless, even better if it's addictive so we buy more... look at her, numbed, no fire, a good little drone doing her homework. That's what plastic food does."

Joseph's dog was crunching and slurping, and Joseph himself sat down heavily at the table, turning sideways as always, only half joining in. "They want to keep kids quiet, don't they?" he said. "Ritalin, TV..."

"But she doesn't even have a TV!" Warren exclaimed, triumphantly. "You can't blame TV for her being a zombie. She's living here with fresh air, wildlife, a garden, no video games... it's food, years and years of junk masquerading as food. Anaesthetic for the soul."

"Hey," said my mum, coyly. "I used to cook proper food, sometimes..." She looked teasingly at Warren, and he responded with a grin.

"You! Cook!"

"Hey, I can cook…"

"Yeah, beans on toast."

"I can cook! I'm not the housewife type, but I can make a lasagne. Not on a woodburner, though..."

"What about on the Aga?"

"I don't know how to use that thing. It's a monster!" She was laughing.

Bernard looked up over his reading glasses. "I used to bake bread in that Aga," he said, in a humour-tipped voice that invited us to express astonishment. He took off his glasses and looked fondly at the bubbling beast. "Yes, I think I'll have a go at baking again one of these days. Mitzi loved my fruitcakes."

My mum and Warren were generally flirtatious with one another when they weren't fighting. Sometimes, when Warren lectured everyone about the war in Iraq, she looked bored and sat resting on her elbow with her hand cupping her mouth and chin. When they had really big fights she sometimes said we were leaving, and shouted at me to pack my stuff. The first time it happened I rushed to pack; I was afraid I would have to leave things behind and I stuffed my belongings into my school bag and sports bag, thinking maybe I could wear all my clothes in layers, and make a bundle rolled up in a sheet... but by then she had forgotten about leaving, and shut Warren out of the bedroom instead. He was in his pants, white and sweaty with sparse black hairs on his chest and shoulders, like a balding dog, shouting at the door and slamming it with the palm of his hand.

"Some people are never happy with what they've chosen," Tori said. She was working in the last of the afternoon light, by the open door of her studio, painting curls on a plate with a pointed brush held in a gloved hand. She had a scarf looped round her face. "Some people never settle; they always think there's something better out there. Maybe they don't trust themselves to have made the right choice. They change their minds, keep moving on, changing jobs, having affairs. They can't love the person they married because they can't believe that they chose the right person."

My father was getting married. I had received an invitation to the wedding. It was printed on thick cream card in a typeface that pretended to be ornate handwriting: 'David and Katherine invite you to Treadwell House on 3 May at 2pm to share their joy in uniting their lives in marriage. Please RSVP by 20 April.'

My mother wanted to see it.

"Bloody pathetic. I give them six months. Look at that - I bet it's all flowers and three-tiered cake, she'll have a white dress like some virgin bride, pathetic. They're drones."

The next day she was laughing about it. "Ooh, David and his blushing bride, the happy couple, hand in hand like the figures on top of the cake."

Then she was angry. "That's where all his bloody money's gone, on a big bloody do for his new wife. Never mind his daughter."

She said I shouldn't go. "Write to him. Send him a letter asking how much the bloody wedding's costing him. Tell him where to stick his bloody invitation."

Then she wanted me to go. "You could make a right bloody stir. Ask her: do you know what he's like? Know what you're letting yourself in for? You could tell her a few things. You could go in rags, go with holes in your shoes, let them all see the way he's keeping his daughter. He's buying champagne while his kid's half-starved. Ask her how much the bloody cake cost."

She had a frenzied row with Warren one night. When they fought in the early hours, in and out of their bedroom on the stairs, it felt as if they were performing, in the centre of the house, while everyone else was lying awake in their dark rooms around the periphery, listening. It was like experimental theatre. Listening carefully, you had to work out what was happening from disjointed sentences, obscure shouts, and ambiguous pauses. "Yes, I do!" my mother wailed, from deep at the bottom of the stairs. "I can't help it! I can't explain it! I'll never stop loving him..." She sobbed on the bottom step, while the whole house lay silent and attentive.

I didn't go to the wedding. I had nothing to wear and no-one to drive me there. Three weeks after, though, my dad picked me up from school and took me out for pizza. We looked strangely formal: me in school uniform, him in his suit, his shirt unbuttoned at the throat and his tie knot askew. It was Friday, and we both had a crumpled, end-of-a-long-week look, as we crawled into a semicircular booth beneath a window overlooking a rush-hour street. We ordered garlic bread and an enormous pizza to share; the waiter had to stretch across it as he rolled the cutting wheel back and forth.

"It was a shame you couldn't be there," my dad said. The garlic bread dripped warm oil over my fingers. "I'd have liked you to have been there."

The napkins were too small and shiny to be of use.

"I'd like you to meet Kate. You'd like her. She'd like you. She wants to meet you."

Outside, the traffic was jolting in the twilight, brake lights all the way up the street and pedestrians swarming across between the cars.

"You know, well, you won't know, but we're going to have a baby. Did you know? Anyway, we are. We're very excited. You'll have a baby brother or sister! Anyway." He was sitting forwards with his fat elbows on the table and his hands meeting, in a triangle. "What I wanted to tell you was this. I've put some money away for you. A decent amount, several thousand, well, six thousand to be exact. What I've done is, I've put it in trust for you; it's a bond, a good rate, eight per cent fixed, really good rate; anyway, it's in trust until you're eighteen. So the idea is, it'll grow, and when you're eighteen you can have it all. It's not for your mother, it's for you. Do you get me?"

"I can have it when I'm eighteen?"

"That's right." He reached for pizza, having said what he wanted to say, and pulled away a drooping slice, trailing elastic cheese. "I suggest you don't tell your mother."

I didn't.

For all my complaining about lack of comforts, in some ways New Gaia was as sublime as it was intended to be. I hadn't appreciated before that I had been growing up in an emphatically urban environment, in streets of uneven terraced houses, dustbins, dog dirt and chewing gum. Around Cross Street, the tarmac roads were patched and the margins crowded with parked cars, while moving cars roared down the narrow corridors between them. Against the constant background wash of traffic were the sounds of children's mocking laughter, drunks under streetlamps and other people's sound systems from open windows. The only wildlife was the jackdaws, coughing from the chimney pots. Now, at New Gaia, I woke up to birdsong, the insistent cooing of wood pigeons and the musical chatter from the garden. In spring the green stuff grew extravagantly and almost daily, as if pixies had come in the night to stick on more leaves and buds; the trees and bushes grew upwards and outwards, thickening and knotting and merging with the long grass into a great uneven green clump, until colourful flowers began to pop out everywhere. And as spring melted into summer it all just kept growing, more lush, more colourful and more musical.

At first, the birds were invisible to my urban eyes: I could hear whole operas of shrill, excited voices, but for all I could tell someone could have concealed speakers in the thickets to fool me; it was Tori who tuned me in to the small, fleeting wildlife, the blackbird diving into the hawthorn with a stuffed beak, the tiny goldfinch broadcasting with incredible volume from a twig at the top of the eucalyptus, and the dozen sparrows tumbling in and out of their rhododendron tower block.

I read *Swallows and Amazons* and Enid Blyton, and felt embraced by the olden days, when teenagers were still called children. I imagined climbing rocks, damming streams and building dens in the undergrowth, camping out under the stars and cooking over an open fire. I imagined a gang of us, in shorts, waking early, swimming in a sparkling lake. It was a world far more welcoming than hair straighteners and *Big Brother*.

By the end of the winter Steve, Paul and Andy had left. The summer brought new people. A cheerful young couple set up a tent in the garden, talked tenaciously about Jesus, and after a while moved on. An artist friend of Joseph's moved in to share his studio, but they fell out after a week and he moved out again. A man came to enquire how we felt about nudists. Layla looked very nervous and Bernard told him genially that we were a mixed bunch from mixed backgrounds and might not all feel comfortable with him as a housemate.

A family, with children younger than me, turned up in a campervan one day. The father was full of enthusiastic ideas. He talked about solar panels and digging out the old pond and organic farming and selling surplus. The children, confident and hostile, wearing bright woven clothes and surly faces, climbed the trees in the garden and stared down at me. They coveted my attic room and their dad made plans to "open up the rest of the attic." They all crowded into my room, and ducked through the open doorway into the darkness, creaking around on the fragile beams and emerging in a cloud of dust and cobwebs.

"Easy!" Their dad said. "We only need to put some boards down, wire up a light... I could put a window in the roof there, I could make a wooden one... and if we get some timber I could make you beds, with tents over them. That'd be fun, wouldn't it? You could all play up here. The whole attic could be for the kids. Kids only, eh?"

They stared at me, dust in their hair, unsmiling. I felt as if someone had stolen all my belongings and was wearing them in front of me. Fortunately, they left as abruptly as they had arrived, packing up their campervan one morning to strike out for a co-operative farm they'd heard of in Cornwall.

A man named Alex arrived with his backpack and beard in early summer, and he sat placidly outside the back door, whittling wood with his penknife. In fine weather some of the others would drag chairs out so they could sit there too, but they would forget to bring them back in. One wet morning Layla was in tears, clattering wooden chairs blindly against the doorframe, until Tori and I arrived to help. Everything about her was drooping and damp: her floating clothes, her bedraggled hair, her crumpled face. She sat sniffing into a tissue while we carried in the chairs. Their wooden frames were dark and slippery from a night of rain, and they were too damp to sit on for a few days. Everyone seemed to think it was someone else's fault.

Alex himself didn't use a kitchen chair, but sat on an upturned bucket or plant pot, or even cross-legged on the ground.

In wet weather, he sat in the kitchen. Warren often sat across from him and made him rooibos tea.

"Anyone can build their own house," Alex would be saying. "You hone your carpentry skills as you go along, learning by doing. I plan to find a patch of woodland nobody wants, get permission from a landowner or maybe even find some genuine wilderness..."

"Common land!" Warren exclaimed, nodding vigorously. "We all have a right to common land."

"...if you build in woodland, then your materials are all around you. A few basic tools and some traditional methods, some rope, some nails... though if you take your time over your mortice joints, you can make a whole house with not an ounce of ironmongery."

"The traditional ways are the best," agreed Warren.

"So you set up in some forgotten wild wood no-one wants, you start in early spring so you've got a good six or eight months before the weather draws in; you chop your trees and split the trunks and build a good frame... you only need a house ten by eight, that's all a man needs, maybe more if you've got a family. And of course you're surrounded by all the firewood you need, for cooking and warmth and light."

"And it keeps growing," added Warren. "Endlessly renewable fuel."

"That's right," said Alex. They sat opposite each other, each with a mug from which a white teabag tag dangled on a thin damp string. I liked the lemon and ginger teabags best. I would be doing my homework while Warren and Alex talked. Sometimes my mother sat with them, interrupting until she got bored and wandered off.

"And for the roof, you make wood shingles," said Alex. Warren made appreciative noises like someone admiring fine food in a restaurant. "Beautiful they are. You get a log -" he gestured with his hands "- and split it, first with an axe, and then with a chisel and mallet, you split it into shingles and to make a waterproof roof you just have to layer them right, carefully overlapping. And you can catch rainwater in a tank and use it for washing and drinking."

"Pure rainwater," put in Warren, "is the best thing you can drink. No chlorine, no fluoride, nothing the government puts in to keep you quiet."

"And for food," said Alex, "you've got your chickens, of course, free range, and your vegetable patch, and you can hunt rabbits."

"Rabbits?" interrupted my mother.

"Yes, rabbits. You eat meat, don't you?"

"Yes, but killing a rabbit yourself, skinning it and all that..."

"It's natural," said Warren. "You should kill and prepare your own food with your own hands. You don't waste it then. You respect it."

"But all that blood and..."

"It's natural. People have always hunted. It's real food."

"You can catch fish too," said Alex. "And birds. Pigeons. And game birds, pheasants, if you were in the right sort of place. You eat what you find, you live in the countryside, truly live in it."

"Away from so-called civilisation," said Warren.

"But you couldn't live completely on your own," objected my mum. "What about clothes, shoes..." She looked around the table. "Cups?"

"You can trade your skills," Alex said. He himself was wearing the green jumper he always wore, with a hole under the arm and a complex smell. "You trade your carpentry work for milk, clothes, shoes... you make someone a table in exchange for a pair of boots. And you don't need much - a cup, a knife, a plate - if you look after them. Good tools should last a lifetime."

He lent me a book to read, a browned paperback copy of *Walden* by Thoreau, a nineteenth century memoir of an American who built himself a house in the woods and lived in a blissful state of self-sufficiency. For me, what was enchanting about the book was the solitude and freedom: Thoreau withdrew from other people and lived alone, in private, doing whatever he wanted, whenever he wanted; it was a world away from the communal living at New

Gaia. The only thing my life had in common with Thoreau's was washing in cold water.

At the end of July, after school had finished, it was Layla's birthday, and we had a party. It was a perfect summer evening, blue and gold, and Bernard was as excited as a child, washing out mugs and glasses from the deepest cupboards. He sent Tori and me to pick basil from the vegetable patch so he could make fresh pesto. The basil grew in little clumps between the overgrown rosemary bushes, and Tori and I snapped handfuls of leaves off the stems. Not all our vegetables had been a success since Andy moved out: the early potatoes had looked wholesome, if knobbly, but when cut into every one was black and hollow inside; the cabbages were shredded by slugs and the garlic didn't grow at all; but the herbs grew aggressively, like weeds, the rosemary and thyme becoming quite woody and the chives flowering purple. Everything made my fingers smell wonderful. Bernard made oily green pesto and oily brown hummus, and set the bowls out on the table with crusty bread and several bottles of wine.

Tori and I carried out the kitchen chairs and arranged them in the patio area. The paving stones were choppy, dislodged by weeds, and the edge of the patio was blurred by overgrown, matted bushes. Tori had made some pottery candle holders, and we equipped them with tealights and set them all around the garden, ready for lighting later. Sunlight glinted on the enormous spiders ' webs and dark pink flowers hung like tiny lanterns from the effusive fuchsia.

Right from the start of the evening, Layla was tightly coiled. Rather innocently, I asked her how old she was when we were in the kitchen together. She didn't look at me, but said," I suppose your mother got you to say that," and walked quickly out of the room. She had earlier left the bathroom sink streaked burgundy with hair dye, and she wore tumbling tassled earrings and a new silky shawl that kept slipping off her shoulders, so that she had to snatch at it inelegantly. When her wine glass was empty she held it by the stem and looked sardonically at Bernard until he jumped up to refill it.

We were all supposed to read poems. Joseph read something short and obscure by an Irish poet, and Bernard stood up dramatically to declaim a sonnet. Tori read out something by TS Elliot; it was a mix of sonorous phrases, simple rhymes, and Latin and German, like someone flicking randomly through TV channels. My mother and Warren had drunk full glasses of wine by then and they sniggered openly. Warren said poetry wasn't their thing but he volunteered me; I had chosen the shortest poem I could find and when it finished abruptly there was a short pause before everyone applauded politely.

Alex read a poem about nature by Walden, and Warren leaned forward with his elbows on his knees and a neutral expression, ignoring my mother, who was trying to catch his eye. Even when she snorted into her wine he didn't look at her. He wouldn't laugh at Alex.

Joseph's dog had got bored and restlessly swivelled around, looking up at each of us in turn while its tail swished mechanically. The wine was finished but Bernard brought out a surprise bottle of schnapps - "Mitzi's favourite". I was encouraged to try some; it tasted very sweet but made my throat clench. Alex was talking about self-sufficiency and a better way of living. Joseph got up to stretch his legs.

As it grew dark, Tori and I lit the candles in their little shallow dishes. If I used a match, the flame reared up to bite my fingers as soon as I tried to point it downwards, so Bernard fetched us some of the tapers that were used to light the woodburner.

Everyone remarked at the pink-streaked sky, changing like a slow kaleidoscope, and as the sunlight became horizontal everything in the garden became less distinct, except for the flames in the candles, which brightened and blossomed.

Tori and I took a walk as far as the rose bush. The small pink flowers were melting into brown mush, and the bush, like everything else in the garden, was wrapped in bindweed and brambles. The brambles projected long gruesome shoots, armed with purple thorns, reaching blindly but hopefully over and above the shrubs; the pale flowers had disintegrated now, and the white petals were caught in the thicket like tiny scraps of paper, revealing hard little green bobbles, the proto-blackberries. The bindweed, its stems delicate but strong as wire, sprouted bold, triangular leaves, and buds which had suddenly and unexpectedly opened to cover everything in big white flowers. Tori heard Warren and Alex calling, and went to see what they wanted; I stayed among the still, darkening vegetation, until it suddenly seemed sinister and sent me scuttling back to the house.

The chairs outside all stood empty and mysterious, and the kitchen was dark. One of Tori's candle holders had been kicked over and split in half. I picked up the pieces, still faintly warm, and looked at the broken edges where the brown glaze showed itself to be just a thin skin over the pale clay inside. The tealight had gone out and spilt melted wax, soft and greasy.

I took the path past the water butt, a big plastic tub bleached from black to silvery grey, propped on a wooden base so rotten that flowers grew from it, alongside an uneven holly bush shot through with brambles and a fulsome patch of buddleia, to come within sight of the polytunnel. There was no breeze, and for once the tattered plastic was silent, but I could hear voices inside, and I walked up to the door. It was gloomy inside, but I could see Bernard holding a tiny glowing roll-up to his mouth. He was sitting in his usual chair, his long legs folded around one another, and as he moved his hand from his mouth to rest on his knee I heard him say," You're just being a bitch."

It was strange to hear Bernard saying the word bitch. He was always so wholesome and mellow, like a vicar or a teacher. Then I heard my mother's voice, her confident drawl like a cartoon snake. "I'm only saying... I mean, where is she now? Joseph disappeared, then *she* disappeared..."

"I don't know what you hope to achieve," said Bernard.

"Well, if you don't want to hear it, that's your business. Roll me one of those, would you?"

I didn't want to hear any more and I moved away from the polytunnel, towards the outbuildings. It was colder now, and although the sky above was still luminous, the garden was dark, clogged with shadows, thick and murky as I moved hesitantly and blinked.

"Amy, is that you?" It was Tori, just outside her studio.

"Yes!" I came close to her. She smelled of woodsmoke and herbs.

"You'll never guess what those idiots are trying to do," she said. I couldn't see her properly but she sounded easygoing, like she was smiling.

"What?"

"Alex and Warren. They've found a hedgehog and they want to cook the poor thing and eat it. Apparently the traditional way to cook a hedgehog is to cover it in clay and put it in a fire. I've told them they're not having any of my clay but they've still gone off to light the woodburner anyway."

"That's horrible," I said.

"Oh, Bernard won't let them do it."

"But Bernard's not in the house - he's in the polytunnel."

"We'd better fetch him then."

We set off in the darkness. My eyes were fumbling, like a swimmer in treacle. The white plastic of the polytunnel had an eerie brightness, although it was still gloomy inside. "Bernard?" called Tori.

There was furtive movement and a gasp. Bernard and my mother were both standing up, moving apart.

"Oh," said Tori, in simple surprise at seeing my mother there, out of context. "Bernard. Could you come to the kitchen? You won't believe what Alex and Warren are up to."

We all processed back to the house. There were candles lit in the kitchen and all the surfaces were emanating the cold of evening. Alex and Warren were there, in the angular, trembling shadows. Bernard and Tori went in, and a noisy conversation erupted, but I stayed in the doorway and realised my mother was still outside, smoking a cigarette. I stepped towards her. She was standing very upright, but employing languid gestures, like someone in a film, and when she raised her cigarette to her lips, between sharp, scissored fingers, the tip glowed brightly in the dark for a resolutely long draw. I stood near her and smelled alcohol. She flicked tiny sparks of ash.

"I've had it with him," she said. I said nothing, afraid to speak in case I accidentally changed her mind. I hated Warren.

"This whole place is shit," she went on. She was speaking quietly but distinctly, rounding every word. "Everyone here is shit. They talk nothing but shit. The whole fucking concept is shit." She wasn't looking at me; in the starlight I could see her eyes glaring at the open kitchen door, beyond which voices prattled and candlelight bobbed. "A shit place full of shits."

Her cigarette glowed again, and in the fierce rush I could see it shorten, as if she was sucking in its fire. She blew smoke through her nose, pale grey and lingering. "And you," she said suddenly. "You can stop hero-worshipping that silly bitch. She's the biggest shit of them all."

She scattered another volley of ash. "As soon as she's asleep, I'm going to smash all her twee fucking pots."

I hated her then. I stood, impotent, in the darkness, and hated her, hated her for always having the last word, and for always being there. She was the one continuous cord in my life, the dingy that carried me along, the one thing that was always there when everything else was lost or crushed or left behind. I hated her.

The nurses had gone. There were some new packages of mysterious medical supplies on the shelves, boxes called Voltec and Zespend in mauve and grey. My mother was tilted by her pillows, like a great ship in dry dock arranged by Lilliputian workers.

The liquid soap above the sink had dripped, puddling a little blob of pale blue antibacterial fluid on the white surface. There was, I noticed, no plug in the sink, so stale water couldn't be inadvertently left there. The water could only gush through and rush away without pausing, sluicing the hands. I looked down at the curved-up edges of the floor and thought that it was as if someone had put paper down so that any mess could be easily scooped, rolled up and binned. The whole room was wipe-clean and disposable.

From time to time there were footsteps passing in the corridor, doors swinging, and voices.

"...that's the thing I said to her, and it was after that..."

106

"What? I thought it was the red one..."

"...take him instead then."

It was only ever part of a sentence, part of a conversation, a voice without a face, footsteps without a body. While I sat here, purposelessly, people went about their busy daily work. I was a visitor in their workplace, a face they would see every day for a few days and then never see again, like all the other visitors' faces. They knew the corridors, the stiffness of the door hinges, the echo of the stairwell; this was their place of work, as familiar as their own bed.

A laundry trolley, like a huge canvas bin on wheels, rolled wearily along outside, and stopped, and I heard clumps of fabric landing inside before it moved slowly off. The large nurse appeared unexpectedly in the doorway, holding on to the doorframe and scanning the room for something forgotten before she saw me and smiled.

"How are we doing?" she said.

"Okay."

"Eaten something?"

"Oh yes, thanks."

"Good, good." We were both looking at my mother now, I from the chair and she from the door, like people distracted by a television set. I looked at my mother, and then back at the nurse. She was watching my mother thoughtfully, her broad crop-nailed hands resting on her bulbous hips, her plump elbows sticking out contentedly. She looked like she was thinking sensible thoughts. After a while she said again," Good, good," looked at me, smiled, and left.

Sometimes it seems that the world is anchored by these large, wise women, women who know everything about life. Women like Alison and Emma at work, or Kate, my dad's wife - women who quietly understand every situation and calmly carry out the correct moves, while I look on, skinny-shouldered and in the way, saying something gauche, witless. There were girls at school who weren't clever or pretty but knew how to tack into the wind; they were graceful beneath the teachers 'smiles, they always had boyfriends, they had always seen the latest episode or heard the latest track and if there was a crisis, a trapped finger or collapsed desk, they were the ones sent by the teacher to find the caretaker or inform the head, or accompany the wounded to the nurse. I could only envy them. They must have been born like that.

My mother was wearing a white nightdress now, with a lacy collar, greyed slightly from overwashing. She might die this evening; perhaps that was why the nurse was looking at her so thoughtfully. Women like that had a feel for the world, an understanding. She would have 'feelings 'about patients and always be ready to do the right thing at the right time. Whereas I would probably be in the canteen, or snoring at home in bed, when the moment of my mother's death finally came.

She had been dying for three days now. I had become so used to her lying there that it felt like she would lie there forever; but of course she had been brought to this room to die.

Her brain was dying like a mobile phone dropped in water, water seeping into the circuits and electronic structures, blood squashing and flushing the delicate chemical fluctuations of neurones and synapses. A fine, complex, microscopically precise apparatus, awash with a simple, brutal fluid. It was like a tsunami washing away a city. Or like a matchstick cathedral, after years of careful crafting, going up in flames.

Footsteps went by; squeaky soles. A voice called after the feet and they hurried back. Something was happening somewhere. I sat alone with my mother, or what was left of her, saying nothing.

When Mark and I went to see her in Acorn Ward, I was afraid of how she would look and how she would behave. I knew she was in a psychiatric ward, of course, but the fact that we were rushing to a hospital in response to sudden events made me think of accidents, blood and bandages. Trauma made everything dark around the edges and distorted in the middle. When we were asked to wait outside I felt that events were happening off-camera, strange and nonsensical events involving my mother. She might be shrieking hysterically, pursued by burly nurses, or weeping on a bed, or sitting at a table swearing across it at a doctor, or hiding, or hurt. My head was cluttered with images of hospital beds, of tubes and flesh, and I felt we were being kept away because something terrible was happening, something so terrible I had to be kept away.

We were literally waiting outside, in the small garden between the corridors. Mark was very calm. "Let's sit down," he said, and we sat on a bench.

"Did you see the knife?" I asked him.

"No, no, I didn't."

"Why do you think she took the knife with her?"

"Oh, you know your mum; being dramatic I suppose. I'm sure she didn't mean to use it."

"Was it one of our kitchen knives?"

"I think so."

"Will the police keep it?"

"I don't know. Maybe."

A young woman in a dressing gown came out into the garden, scowling at the ground. She sat on the other bench.

"Did you see her letters? I mean the ones the police have got?"

"No, I didn't see them. The sergeant just gave me an idea of what was in them."

"Were they really threatening letters?"

"Well, yes, but I don't think she meant any of the threats. You know your mum: she got carried away."

That was when I told him about Lucas Street, and the fire. And then he put his arm around me, and it felt good.

I wondered if she was making a scene, running rampant in the hospital, being restrained. She seemed so big and uncontained, capable of anything.

And yet here she was now, in this hospital bed, draining away quietly. Unconscious in a small room, wearing someone else's nightgown.

I shouldn't be caught by surprise by the natural order of life. We are all born, and find ourselves children in a world of adults, buffeted about and helpless. Then one day we become adults ourselves, and those omnipotent parents become weak and die, while we step up to their place, have offspring of our own and walk in adult shoes until we, too, are replaced. And yet it was a shock to me to realise that I had become an adult, and my mother was no longer the mother of a child.

It makes no sense, really. Childhood feels like a state of existence, not a phase. Although life is all change and transition - a movement through time where the minute past is already gone and we are already different - we feel ourselves to be static and permanent. A person exists in a perpetual present: if Jane Smith is a woman with brown hair and a toothy smile, it makes no sense to say that Jane Smith is also a little girl with gaps for teeth or an old woman with grey in her hair. And yet Jane Smith is all of those people. My mother was a child once, a newborn baby; all that separates her then and her now is time, intangible and ridiculous.

She was still breathing, although she looked more faded now. Perhaps it was the worn-out nightgown, suggesting weariness. When I was very small, I hated bedtime, because the end of every day seemed like a kind of death. I hated the drawn-out routine of bath, pyjamas, those suffocating storybooks - it was like being slowly smothered. How much more dreadful is the deathbed scene, the slow theatre of dying. The stifling dignity, the clichés, the waiting.

Deathbed scenes are like courtroom scenes, bloated with self-importance, crushing the actors. Once begun, the process is unstoppable, irreversible.

Often, at court, a defendant who is waiting for a verdict, guilty or not guilty, fidgets nervously and says: "I just want to get it over with. I don't care what they decide. I just want to know one way or the other." But is it really better to know than to wait? Which is worse: the state of limbo outside the courtroom door, or the finality of a guilty verdict and a prison sentence, a door that slams shut? Isn't it better to hang in a perpetual present of uncertainty, than to drop into an irrevocable ending?

Thursday

There was consternation in the hospital car park. The barrier wouldn't open. The queue had become hot and edgy; some cars had bumped up onto the curb, threatening the stunted shrubs that grew among the bark chips; some people had unrolled windows or even got out, talking to each other randomly.

"The ticket machine isn't working. He says someone's gone for help."

"It won't go up. It's showing some kind of error code."

"You can't go in through the exit. They've got those things that burst your tyres."

It was a fine morning, and everyone was enjoying open windows and shirt sleeves, in spite of their twitchiness at the sight of so many empty parking spaces taunting them from beyond the thin horizontal arm. Car doors opened and closed and voices called from warm interiors. A woman stopped at the car in front of me and leaned on a stranger's window to laugh with him at the absurdity of modern life. Finally a man in a bright yellow vest turned up with some tools and dismantled the side of the ticket machine, squatting uncomfortably in his steel-toed boots. He exposed the disordered wiry entrails of the sleek machine and after some digging about he stood up and operated the barrier with one finger on a hidden button so we could all drive through. There was to be no charge today, and everyone was suddenly smiling, like children when the school is unexpectedly closed.

On my way into the building I took my phone out and saw there was a message. I immediately thought that my mother had died while I was on my way here, while I was dawdling at traffic lights, sitting in the sun, choosing a track on the CD. But the voice was Alison's.

111

"Hi there, it's Alison - could you give me a ring when you've got a minute? No hurry, nothing to worry about."

I wondered if maybe they had lost some paperwork, or I had lost some paperwork and they had found out that I'd lost it, and I was worrying about work as I wandered into my mother's room.

She was still there, still alive, and my chair was still there, and I sat down and looked at her. I could hear the morphine machine humming with a gentle rise and fall, in and out like a robot breathing, and the coarser breaths of my mother, just as steady but noisier and human. They weren't quite synchronised.

My mother always had a certain gesture, a way of narrowing her eyes when she was thinking. She would look away into the distance, and the muscles around her eyes would squeeze, as if she was squinting into binoculars, or fighting against a bright light. I remember, when I was very little, I used to try to imitate the movement myself, to see what it felt like. Watching her, I narrowed my own eyes, blurring the world. It made my eyes tickle and I had to rub them back to normal.

I think that was when I realised the impossibility of understanding another person. We don't just die alone, we live alone, strangers to one another.

My college friends and I used to talk, when we were drinking, about how little our parents understood us. We were complicated and emotional; parents were simple and self-satisfied. We saw all the messy possibilities of life while they followed their neat paths and fences. The Shakespeare pub in town was famous for underage drinking, and we squeezed into seats underneath the widescreen TV and peeled the paper layers off beer mats while we drank rum and coke and talked about our unbearable families.

"God, it's like I'm an alien," Elena would say, as we bumped elbows in the small space. "You won't believe what my dad said..." As we drank round after round, the lights and sounds brightened and the faces became sharper and quicker. I wondered aloud what it meant to understand someone. Elena said it was about acceptance; Charlotte said you had to think the same way, speak the same language, be on the same wavelength. Can you love someone even if you don't understand them? As with all drunken

112

conversations, it felt as if I was touching the edge of an enormous, beautiful insight, but my reaching fingers only pushed it further away.

Of course, my college friends were all enormously impressed by my shocking family life. Having a psychiatrically suspect mother was very cool, and I regularly told the story of her admission to Acorn Ward, her brush with the police, our outlandish life back at New Gaia and even our days in bed and breakfast accommodation at Willow House, when we were officially homeless, after the fire in Lucas Street. At school I had been the strange, smelly girl, but at sixth form college I was cool. My friends 'parents all washed their cars and went to zumba and held dinner parties. I lived in a caravan.

We had been living at the Green Meadows Caravan Park, on and off, for years, ever since we left New Gaia. There was a year or so when we lived with Mark, but Mum always kept the rent up on the caravan, so she had a place to storm off to. By the time I was in college she had walked out on Mark, and we were back in the caravan, but she still cried after a few drinks and said she was a fool for leaving her rock. Mark was always her rock, even when she was sick of him, and even when she walked out on him there was always the possibility that she would walk back. The caravan was the perfect home; it kept her options open.

When we first moved to the Green Meadows Caravan Park we unlocked our caravan to find an interior that had slipped out of time, as if a spell had been cast in the seventies to send everything into an enchanted sleep. The fittings of the kitchen, the brown lino, the patterned sofa and the teak-veneer wood were all in perfect condition, as if untouched for decades, free from dust or mildew. I suspected the caravan had been occupied by an old person who had died, but I didn't want to ask. There were two tiny bedrooms. Mine had a bed built of thick cushions on top of a deep storage box, and it wasn't quite the length or width of a real bed; there was a fitted wardrobe, too, narrow and oddly shaped. The kitchen had a two-ring gas hob connected to an orange canister outside, and we had mains water and electricity.

113

All the other residents of the caravan park were elderly people. They were small and white-haired, and because I was the only young person on the site they brightened when they saw me and came over like dwarves drawn to Snow White. I half expected them to stroke my hair. "Oh, good afternoon, dear, did you have a lovely day at school?" All their questions were about school, and they loved my uniform. "You do look smart in that blazer, dear." Most of them had small irritable dogs on long leads.

Their caravans were kept beautifully. Although they were born with wheels, they had all been boxed in around their bases with bricks or white-painted concrete blocks, so that they looked like little bungalows. Their wheels were shackled. Often the low brick walls were extended to form raised flower beds and there were miniature trees, gnomes, and woodland creatures made of stone. The prettiest caravans had fake wooden shutters and lantern-style lamps above the doors, and most had names like Travellers Rest or Golden Sunset. One was covered with multicoloured oversized butterflies made of nylon. There were gravel paths and small, brightly-coloured cars with very low mileages.

My mother hated the old people. "Shoot me before I get old," she said.

The site was owned and run by Reg from his office, an odd building at the entrance which seemed to have been built from leftovers of UPVC windows and panels. Reg was a stringy man with a severely weatherbeaten face and a boxy Land Rover, more like a shed than a car, which he left unlocked when he drove up to the office at an angle and jumped out. He had crooked teeth and when he spoke they occasionally made sharp whistling noises. It was fascinating, and made it difficult to listen to what he was saying.

The front of the office was encrusted with notices on plywood boards. No Through Road. No Unauthorised Parking. Vehicles Will Be Clamped. Hawkers Beware: Police Will Be Called Immediately. All the notices were painted in big black letters on white, except one, which was crowded with tiny print, hard to read even if you stood right in front of the office. It was a list of rules, written by someone who had thought of everything that could possibly need to be prohibited, from campfires to leylandii.

Most of the caravans had steps built of brick up to their front doors, but we had a flimsy metal stepladder that clanged when you walked up its three steps. Barbara, from the caravan next door, told us we ought to get some proper steps built. "You need to get that aerial looked at too, before it falls on someone's head!" Our TV aerial tilted as if it was trying to reach across to its sturdier friend on Barbara's roof. "I'll get my son to look at it for you," she said. "And you'll need some net curtains putting up, too!"

Barbara was a jolly little woman in polyester trousers and vivid patterned cardigans, her bony ankles dipped into fluffy slippers and a heavy pendant swinging from her sinewy neck. She lured us into her caravan for tea and marshmallow teacakes, big chocolate-coated globes of goo that exploded stickily all over my face and fingers. She served tea in cups with saucers, and offered us a bowl of sugar cubes. "Go on," she twinkled, "have another teacake."

Her sitting room was like a proper room in a house. Walking in through the caravan door was disconcerting, like walking on to a film set. There were china ornaments in a glass cabinet, shelves cluttered with photographs in silver frames and a dark wood fireplace surround cradling an electric fire and glittering with horse brasses. She even had a parrot in a cage. It was grey, with an unexpected red tail, and it didn't talk but made a comical noise like a penny whistle. When we visited, it climbed steadily up and down the side of its cage, using its beak as a third limb, reaching and grasping as deliberately as a gymnast practising on wall bars.

"My son put that picture up for me, do you like it?" Barbara asked. She didn't wait for an answer. "I just love sunsets, all that orange. My son was over last Saturday, he's so helpful, a lovely man, and he's been through so much. He married a lovely girl, but she died, you know; she was only thirty-four." We did know, because Barbara had told us before. "Oh, it was an awful thing, awful. She had a lymphoma, that's a type of cancer, awful it was, to see her fade away like that, so young. And my son, he loved her so much, such a tragedy for him, devastated... and they never had children. I'd have loved grandchildren." She looked at me with a hungry look.

We moved into the caravan in late autumn, and we were quickly aware that we needed to prepare defences against winter. Barbara talked of battening down the hatches and securing the property. She warned us of high winds and horizontal rain. She told us stories of snow lying thick and heavy on caravan roofs, and then melting and trickling through cracks like mountain streams, dripping into buckets and darkening carpets. She told us of the cold, of woolly hats worn in bed and frost on the inside of windows and electric bar heaters on all night. Her son had fitted a carbon dioxide detector for her, she said. My mother suggested it was probably carbon monoxide and Barbara just waved the air. "Oh, I don't know," she said, "my son deals with all that for me." She said she would send him round to fit a carbon dioxide detector for us.

When the wind rushed the caravan at night, everything quivered. The door rattled and the thin panels of the walls were sucked in and out, flexing, with a noise like oversized sheets of tinfoil being folded. It felt as if the whole caravan would be lifted up and swirled away. I remembered my Polly Pocket dolls in their little house that was really a plastic purse, and it felt that our caravan was as small and helpless and ridiculous as a house as theirs. As the winter came down over us, the wind barged the walls and the rain rang the roof, and the cold marched in and settled.

My bed was like a bunk in a boat. In itself it was cosy: short, narrow and lumpy, it cocooned me in my sleeping bag and blankets; but it seemed as if the boat itself was exposed on a wide ocean, knocked about in the darkness. Sometimes a jolt from outside would fling open my wardrobe door, or the wind would twist and fire a volley of rain at my window. The whole caravan rocked.

One night our television aerial came down. My mother had bought us a digital box, because the fat little television in the caravan was an old-fashioned analogue one, and we had warmed to the habit, in the evenings, of swaddling ourselves in cardigans on the sofa and allowing ourselves to be fed tragic news, outlandish drama and unlikely comedy until it was so late it was hard to rouse ourselves enough to go to bed. We heard a noise in the night like a leviathan in chains dragging across the roof, and in the early light we put coats over our layers of pyjamas and went outside. The gangly aerial was hanging by its cords, having dented the smooth yellow ripples of the caravan on its way down.

Barbara was already up and fully dressed, approaching gingerly through the wet grass in dainty shoes. "I thought it was that!" she exclaimed, raising her voice to send it ahead of her careful footsteps. "I heard the most dreadful noise..." Fortunately for us, she said, her son was coming for Sunday lunch today and he would fix it for us.

My mother put her clothes on and went up to the office to speak to Reg. She came back in a temper, relating that the toothless old bastard wouldn't do anything, said it had nothing to do with him. She switched on the television and rather unnecessarily flicked through the static. "Fucking hell," she said.

We were beginning to comprehend that everywhere else we had lived there had been people who took care of things that were broken or stuck, people who changed light bulbs and bought bin liners. We hadn't even realised. We had lived like guests for years.

"We don't even have a fucking ladder," my mum said, after a while. "Or a screwdriver."

Eventually there was a tap on the door and we opened it to Barbara, shadowed by an affable man with thinning hair and a toolbox.

"This is my son," she announced.

"Hi," he said, smiling and reaching forward to shake my mum's hand. "I'm Mark."

I went out of the ward, into the main corridor, to return Alison's call.

There was a woman sitting, alone, in a wheelchair aligned with the wall, wearing a dressing gown. She looked very uncomfortable about being in a corridor in a dressing gown. Some people in normal clothes and shoes rumbled past. Her feet were bare, pale and bony with yellow nails, fidgeting against the grey plastic footrest of the wheelchair. I walked on beyond her, so I wasn't looking at her.

I rang work and asked to speak to Alison. I waited, and was put on hold; classical music rang out at an awkward volume. I didn't know we played classical music at people when we put them on hold.

After a while Alison came to the phone. At first she seemed to have forgotten why she had rung me. Alison carried a hundred thoughts in her head at once, spilling them at people as she hurried past. She called it multitasking.

"Oh yes, of course," she said. "Thank you for calling me back... yes, well, it's nothing to worry about, I know you've got a lot to deal with, but I thought I'd better let you know sooner rather than later; I mean, well, everyone knows now so it's only fair; well, you know there have been cuts coming down the line, well, we may have to cut you down to four days a week. It's looking like none of the ushers will be full-time, well, practically none... I just thought I'd tell you now, I didn't want you to hear it from anyone else, you know; anyway, you don't need to do anything, don't need to think about it now. I know you've got a lot on your mind."

I thanked her and said goodbye.

My life was there, at the court, where she was - I could picture her in the office, putting down the receiver and turning to the computer screen - but it felt far away now, as if I were in another country or another time zone. I felt like I was at a foreign airport beside a rickety old phone box, feeding in unfamiliar coins in an attempt to make contact with home, hearing only a crackling, whistling line and a muffled, misshapen voice.

The woman in the wheelchair was trundled past me by a porter. She was clutching the arm rests. There were some nurses laughing at the end of the corridor. It was warm in the hospital, the sunshine through the windows casting huge yellow shapes on the floor.

I walked down the corridor, and the nurses parted to let me swing through the double doors. They looked comfortable in their pale blue uniforms and flat shoes, and I had a sudden longing for my black gown and old-fashioned clipboard. At work I stand in the corridor with my list of names and they come to me to be marked off; I nod and tick their names and acknowledge that they have answered their bail by reporting to me. I tell them where to sit and wait. By ticking off their names I have put them in the system, registered them as present, processed them through to the next stage.

The next corridor was also bright in the sun, and I followed the familiar route to the canteen. I had a nebulous urge to call Alison back, and make contact again with my normal life. She would, of course, be horrified if I did call; she would back away verbally, dropping obstacles as she went, to prevent me from getting close enough to ask a direct question. She might even be too busy to come to the phone, and wave a message across the room. She was never particularly comfortable talking to me anyway.

Viewing my life from here, it looked so small and shut in. My little old house, the neighbours whose names I don't know; if we pass at our front doors I rush out a startled hello and fumble with my keys. My job, my routines, my black gown. I am separate from the other ushers, with their talk of bunions and grandchildren, and separate from the office staff, with their talk of school trips and headlice. I don't chat with anyone. Emma is my friend because she is everyone's friend. She sometimes bundles me out to the pub to meet more people, and I sit behind my drink and watch them laughing. Emma is nice to me because she thinks I'm lonely and odd. After work I go home to my little old house, change into softer clothes, eat food, watch television. I put the heating on when it gets chilly and draw the curtains when it gets dark. I put the recycling out every other Thursday and go to Tesco with my reusable bags every Tuesday after work, when it's quiet.

I don't know how to live any other way. People on television live bright, busy lives, dating, eating in restaurants, serving breakfast to their kids as they check their emails, walking dogs on winter beaches, taking dance classes, gossiping with friends over coffee. They go camping in France and sing in amateur choirs and learn to surf.

Perhaps I just don't live in that kind of TV world. Perhaps I live in a grey foreign language film set in a cold war eastern bloc country, where I betrayed my mother to the secret police and now live in a blank-walled apartment for one and work for the justice system.

119

The stoical lunch queue at the canteen seemed symbolic, perhaps because I had been thinking about the meaninglessness of life. It reminded me of a science fiction film I saw, in which aliens treated human beings like cattle. We were lining up with our trays, shuffling patiently, waiting for our turn at the trough. The canteen staff were still laying out receptacles of cottage pie and pulled pork under the greasy low spotlights, their hands wrapped in overworked teatowels against the hot steel. A man at the front of the queue was smiling down at the cottage pie while the woman in a white hat and apron gouged into it with a giant spoon to give him the first helping.

When my turn came I asked for mediterranean vegetable soup. The woman opened the fat shiny tureen and steam rose from the oily surface of the liquid. She ladled me a bowlful, red and splashing, and I took a bread roll from the basket, scattering poppy seeds.

The sky behind the windows was a smooth, luminous blue, and warmth radiated from the broad glass as much as from my soup. I took off my cardigan and ate in short sleeves, bare elbows on the table as I ripped my bread roll and flung seeds and crumbs across the smooth clean surface.

There's a solicitor who I see at court, a married man in his thirties, who glides confidently in and out of the building and skims across to me to ask if his clients have arrived. He banters with everyone, even me, and our encounters are vaguely unreal, as if we're in a sharply written television drama. I feel self-conscious, and conscious of him, too, from the smell of his well-cut suits to the thick dark fringe of hair that brushes his eyebrows when he raises them humorously; our postures are perfect and even the courtroom corridor looks like a film set. When he walks away, I'm left with a warm, tight feeling that takes time to slacken, and I wonder if he feels the intensity of our conversations, or if his whole life is like that, all his encounters as charged as his encounters with me.

He mentions his wife but he doesn't mention children. He's not good-looking in an obvious way, but dark-haired, with perfect skin and a face that quivers on the edge of laughter. But of course our script has already been written: our roles are co-workers, acquaintances, people who exchange witticisms at nine o'clock on a Monday morning, nothing more.

My life is so small. And if my working hours are cut down to four days, my life will be cut down even smaller. I make such a small mark on the world; as if I'm compensating for the massive scorch made by my mother.

I had to tip my bowl to scrape out the last of the soup. The canteen was becoming too warm in the sunlight, the afternoon swelling and people discarding jackets. I picked up my cardigan and set off back to my mother's bedside.

When my mother and Mark went out together, we stayed over at Mark's house. I watched his TV and did my homework on his coffee table, and he left me bags of crisps or chocolate bars. Sometimes he said we should all go out, which meant I was invited too, and we went to his favourite cinema. The cinema was beautiful, red and gold, awash with carpet: the floor, walls, partitions and seats were all flooded with velvety fabric, speckled in places with black holes from the days when people were allowed to smoke. I loved the moment when the lights went down and the audience shuffled and quietened, and I pressed myself back into the bowed seat and let the movie surge out and take me.

I loved, too, the sensation of coming out of the cinema afterwards, into cold darkness, or shocking daylight in summer. If the film was vivid enough, the world outside would glow, and for a while I felt as if I was still connected to the world in the film. An action movie would make me feel powerful and athletic; a thriller left me clever and cunning; a drama would make the world seem smooth and beautiful, every sight and sound symbolic and meaningful, every word spoken profound and significant.

After a film we went for fast food. We sat under harsh lights at plastic tables and ate out of paper and cardboard packaging. All three of us would be smiling and bubbling, happy and witty. The food was salty and greasy, the drinks heavy with ice. People who saw us thought we were a family.

121

Mum always said to Mark: "Do you want my slice of slug?" She meant the gherkin from her burger, exposed and dripping ketchup when she lifted the smooth lid of the bun.

"Don't mind if I do," he said. "Extra French fries?"

"Venezuelan vinegar?"

"Cantonese ketchup?"

"Sicilian salt?"

On Sundays, Barbara cooked a roast for us all in her caravan. She folded out a precarious table and wedged in four proper dining chairs. I had to slide into my seat sideways because there was no space to pull it back, and my plate weighed down a slanted leaf of apparently unsupported table, so I always ate hastily. Barbara pressed second helpings on me. There wasn't quite enough space on the table for all the serving bowls, so we were continually passing round the carrots or potatoes, like an unending game of musical chairs, although Mark called it pass the parcel. "Can't I tempt anyone to more gravy?" he pleaded, my mother laughing and telling him that if he couldn't find a place for the jug he'd have to drink it. Barbara liked to tell everyone, approvingly, that I ate like a horse. Mark said it was a good thing I didn't smell like one.

Right from the start, though, even as she was falling in love, my mother found Mark irritating. She couldn't love anyone or anything uncomplicatedly; nothing fitted her perfectly, and she picked and ripped at the imperfections. She could never be a contented person, settling herself around life's obstacles, accepting rough edges and cracks. Instead, she was impelled to test every flaw and pull every loose thread, worrying at life, never at rest. Of course, if pulling a loose thread made the whole thing unravel, she would weep for what she had lost.

"You're so bloody boring!" she shouted at Mark, one night after too much wine. "Always going on about bloody DIY!"

DIY was how Mark governed his world. He made plans: after Christmas I'm going to paint those window frames; in March I'll replace the patio. His future was carefully laid out several months in advance. Changes could be made - were, in fact, inevitable, a happy part of the ongoing process of perpetual planning - but the

122

future was never blank, or flat: it was solid, built up, full. He could look ahead and see it.

The past was the same, written into the things around him: I put that shed up in 2012; I painted the kitchen last summer. The past and future were evidenced in the solid objects around him.

He saw time, steady and predictable, in the gentle deterioration of timber and paintwork, in floors becoming worn and roofs becoming mossy, and he could restrain time with his regular work. "Maintaining the house," he called it. "I have to maintain the house," he said to my mum in surprise, as if it were as obvious as breathing, this methodical programme of repair and renewal.

It was a nice house, very clean and neat, painted in soft colours and furnished with oversized cushions. When Mum and Mark went out we stayed over, and slowly the spare room became my room. It was a small second bedroom, a child's room that had never belonged to a child: there were boxes stacked high, a folded ironing board, upended suitcases and a vacuum cleaner bound in its tight cable. The single bed shrank against the wall, as incongruous as a bed in a forest or a workshop. Mark had bought new bedding for me, in sunny colours, and it felt fresh, coarse and superclean. The lampshade cast a huge round shadow on the ceiling.

"Over Easter," Mark said, "I'll clear out the spare room a bit, make it into a proper room for Amy." My mum, pleased by this token of commitment, curled up against him on the sofa like a cat. On Good Friday he cleared out my room and painted it Praline White, and his house became my house, where my clothes hung from a rail and my shoes and diary were stuffed under the bed. We had moved in. I ate breakfast at the table in his kitchen, between his neat stacks of bills and junk mail, and if it was raining he drove me to school before he went to work, the squeaky wipers leaving streaky arcs on the windscreen as he found a spot to pull over so I could jump out, squinting into the swirling wet wind and yelling goodbye as I slammed the door.

I started coming home for lunch. It was a twenty-five minute walk, so from unlocking the front door I had exactly ten minutes to prepare my lunch and consume it before I had to leave again, but it was worth it to escape school, to escape the sly girls and idiot boys. As I walked, quick and free, I planned the ten minutes tactically in my mind: one minute to fill the kettle and switch it on, one minute to put bread in the toaster; get out the mug, plate, milk, butter, everything laid out regimentally ready for the growling kettle to snap off and the toast to leap triumphantly. The first five minutes would be gone. Teabag, milk, cold water frothing into the tea from the tap to make it instantly drinkable; eat standing up, spraying crumbs, enjoying the crispness and the warm melting butter. I could wash up when I came home later. Everything in the sink, brushing off my hands, time to go.

If I had something special planned - a bar of chocolate or a cup of instant soup - I enjoyed preparing my strategy, calculating how I would fit it into my ten minutes, devising the most efficient method for each tiny task; I planned exactly how I would take out a mug and spoon, tear the soup sachet and tap all the powder into the mug while the kettle boiled, my movements like a choreographed dance. My ten minutes were my precious, sanctified time, alone in the kitchen, ten perfect minutes in the middle of every ordinary day.

At school I went into Year Ten; we were studying optional subjects, and often with different classmates for different lessons. Sally had stopped talking to me altogether. A girl called Sydney sat next to me in Spanish, but she ignored me in Maths and Science, when she had her real friends to talk to. English was my best subject, and I was in a class with geeky girls who didn't care who sat beside them. They wrote long, beautiful essays and talked obsessively about old exam papers.

I never had a boyfriend at school, but there was one boy I noticed, a boy named Lucas. He was so ordinary that in school he was almost camouflaged, but I saw him. Everyone else fancied Joshua, blond and broad-shouldered and languidly funny; Lucas was on the periphery of Joshua's circle, the small, good-natured one who could safely be teased. He was quiet and a little awkward. He had dark hair, though not dark enough to be interesting, and light eyes, though not light enough to be striking, and his face was quite angular, his nose a sharp line from bridge to tip, his skin pale and shadowy beneath the eyes. Most of the time he had a slightly

124

nervous look, but very occasionally, when he was unusually relaxed and confident, he smiled, and he was suddenly breathtaking. It was a proper grin, the grin of a clean-cut boy in an Enid Blyton adventure, and I wished I could mentally photograph him and hold that picture in my head forever.

I imagined that I was a film director, casting him in a film. I imagined putting him in the role of a hesitant vampire, tormented by his own nature. I cast him as a reluctant superhero, steeling himself for his first battle. I set him in an alien landscape, crawling, coughing, from his crashed spaceship, clawing out of his bulky spacesuit. I pictured myself, one day, as a famous film director, and him as a struggling actor; I told him I remembered him from our schooldays and he was perfect for a part in my new historical drama. He was profusely grateful, and while stylists ruffled his hair and tightened his collar he listened seriously to my instructions as to how he was to shyly approach the heroine and then break into an unexpected grin.

I thought about him all the time, but I never spoke to him.

At Christmas, we went to Barbara's caravan for lunch. The interior twinkled with red and gold tinsel and multicoloured lights that swaddled a small plastic tree. Even the parrot was excited, hooting and clattering about in his cage so much that Barbara had to put him under a blanket in the bedroom. Mark and my mum grew red faced from wine and I was sweaty from salty gravy and greasy roast potatoes. The television was on, small but loud, and Mum went across to our caravan to pick up our mail. After a while Mark sleepily wondered why she was taking so long, but he was stretched out, long-legged in red socks and mesmerised by the TV, so I said I would go after her.

Outside it was not a white Christmas but a drizzly one: there was a fine rain, almost invisible to my eyes in the grey light but enough to dampen my hair. There was a robin singing somewhere and I could see lights in most of the caravans and condensation in some of the windows. One caravan was pinned all over with blue lights and a neon reindeer, but the others were ignoring it discreetly. Our caravan was dark. I clanged up the stairs and went in.

My mother was standing in the middle of the cold living room with her back to me, looking at the lit face of her phone. "Bastard," she said. Then she heard me and turned round, and without lifting her frown she said: "Can I use your phone?"

I handed her my phone and she said she'd come back over to Barbara's in a few minutes, and could I put the kettle on, so I went back out into the drizzle, the neon reindeer leering at me as I hurried back to the warm, twinkling lights of Barbara's caravan.

A few days later, I got a text. It said: 'Is this U? 'I didn't recognise the number and I deleted it. Later that day there was another one. 'Did U mean wot U said? 'I showed my mum. Mark was at work but she and I were at home, in his house; she was watching a film and I had been daydreaming in my room, listening to music through ear buds. She looked at the text and her eyes narrowed as she thought, and smiled.

"Don't worry about it," she said, and handed me back the phone. "It's nothing."

I didn't receive any more texts and I forgot about them. She always had secrets and schemes, probably more than I ever knew.

My mother's room was warm, even with the door open; the whole ward had a swollen, suffocating feel as the hot weather took the heating system by surprise. One of the nurses was propping open doors and fanning herself with an envelope. I wondered if my mother's body would still sweat even though she wasn't conscious of the heat. The human body has so many unconscious, mechanical systems: heartbeat, breathing, sweating. How much of ourselves do we really know?

After sitting for a while, I realised that the window could be opened. One panel of it had a cunning hinge that would allow it to be swung open just a few inches, far enough to let the breeze come in without anyone throwing themselves out. I got up and walked around the bed to jerk it open.

I hadn't walked up to the window before, and from the other side of the room, where I sat, it framed only sky, so it was a shock to look down and see the busy car park. The hospital was a sprawling, disorientating building, a spill of different architectural styles built at different dates, with connecting walkways and

126

extensions at different levels, all sewn together by the colour-coded corridors, so that from the inside it was impossible to keep hold of a mental map. From the window of this quiet, sombre room I could now see the workaday flurry of the car park. There was a woman trying to open her car door without bumping the vehicle parked too close alongside, and a young man helping a stiff elderly man move achingly slowly in front of waiting traffic. It appeared that the barrier had been fixed, and cars were coming and going, shuffling in and out, swinging too fast round corners, easing into spaces. As I watched, two cars reversed at cross purposes at the same time, and began an ungainly, jolting dance to avoid one other.

If my mother had been conscious, she would still have been unable, from the bed, to see the car park. The only view from the bed was of a square of impassive blue sky. I stood at the window and looked back at her, and the small, impersonal room. It was sad that she was dying in a small room with all that big world outside. But maybe dying is always like that, being left behind. Maybe dying is like slowing down and coming to a standstill while everyone else keeps moving, like giving up in a race. All the activity keeps going, rushing on ahead, leaving you, tired and panting, in the silent dusty road.

"You'll ruin your shoes," Mark used to say to me, but he said it kindly. I stamped my feet in and out of my trainers, too impatient to undo the laces. He always tied his shoes carefully, sitting on the bottom step.

He was a careful person. He unplugged everything at night. He left the keys in the front door, and cleared the shoes from the hall, in case we had to get out of the house in an emergency in the dark. He moved the television away from the radiator so it wouldn't get too warm, wiped down the bathroom tiles after every shower to stop black mould, and put the lights on if we went out in the evening, so that burglars would think we were in. My mum called him a silly sod.

The day she ended up in the psychiatric ward was a Saturday. Mark had made us bacon and eggs, and then he set about cleaning all the speckled grease off the hob and worktops, scrubbing happily in the kitchen with the radio on. My mum said she was bored and going out to the shops, although she didn't invite me to come with her. I settled down to watch a DVD.

As the day tipped over into afternoon Mark started to wonder aloud whether she would come back for lunch, and we both agreed that the enormous breakfast had filled us all up. Mark made us both a cup of tea and when I came into the kitchen he said we could treat ourselves to a proper piggy day and he opened a packet of biscuits. They were chocolate digestives and I remember the mulch of them sticking to my back teeth after I'd finished. I think I had my finger in my mouth, digging at my molars, when there was a knock on the door.

It was the front door, and I heard Mark talking to a man with a deep, important voice, and I looked down the hall and saw he was a policeman. I suppose a policeman at the door is a universal sign of disaster, a sight that sets the pulse racing. The worst of it was that the policeman saw me and then said to Mark: "Can we speak privately?"

I sat on the stairs, halfway up, while they went into the kitchen and shut the door. I could hear voices but not what they were saying. There must have been an accident. Was she dead? I was in a limbo of not knowing, a non-existence between before and after, my life suspended while I waited to find out. I loved her, I couldn't imagine life without her, I couldn't live without her. And if she was dead, who would look after me? My mother was everything; there was just her and me. I was only living in Mark's house because of her; without her, Mark and I were strangers. This wasn't my house. I sat on the stairs with my thoughts opening up beneath me until they came so quickly I couldn't think them, and I just sat there above a great abyss. Then the kitchen door was flung open.

The policeman nodded to me as he left, but Mark turned from closing the door and came straight to me with his palms outstretched and a gentle smile. "It's okay, it's okay," he said. "She's not hurt, she's fine. She's just got herself into a bit of trouble, that's all."

I had to find my shoes and coat so we could set off in the car at once, and Mark went calmly round the house switching everything off, as he usually did, and as we were driving to the hospital he told me what the policeman had said. "She's just got into a pickle," he explained. Apparently she had started seeing Warren again. It wasn't clear whether Warren had contacted her first or she had contacted him, but the police said that, in any case, they had resumed the "tempestuous relationship" that they had had previously.

"I suppose you know more about that than I do," said Mark.

"Warren was horrible," I said. I was surprised at how young I sounded, like a tearful little girl talking about a mean little boy. Mark changed gear and turned onto the main road.

"Well, according to him, they argued, and she started to send him unpleasant texts, and then quite threatening letters. He says that he told her to leave him alone but she kept harassing him, and sending him nasty letters, and then today she turned up at his place with a knife."

"A knife?"

"It's okay, no-one was hurt. It all sounds a bit overdramatic really. You know your mum. Anyway, this Warren bloke called the police and they arrested her, but she was in such a state that they took her to the hospital, to the psychiatric unit. They've handed her over to the doctors there."

He drove steadily to the hospital, as careful as ever, using his mirrors and signals diligently. I felt heightened, aware of the passing scenery as splashes of light and movement: a man with a dog, a tree, an open window; a series of resonant but meaningless images that fell away before I could think about them. My mother had been taken to a psychiatric ward. I wasn't sure if the dramatic events were ending or just beginning. What would a psychiatrist make of her? I had read so widely and familiarly about borderline personality disorder, dysphoria, kleptomania... Perhaps they had clever tests, tricks to catch her in conversation; she would reveal her paranoia or narcissism or mania and the psychiatrist, poker-faced, would make a little note on his pad. Perhaps they would medicate her, with tranquillisers or lithium or Prozac, and she would be tamed and strangely subdued.

I believed, that day, in Mark's car, on that strange, steady journey, that my life had changed, something had snapped, and nothing would ever be the same.

I was wrong. We were sent to wait in the little garden beside Acorn Ward, hemmed in by the wards and corridors, enclosed on all four sides but open to the sky, and after we had been sitting on the bench, talking, for a long time, my mother abruptly appeared at the door, and came striding over to us. I had vaguely and irrationally thought she would be wearing a dressing gown or some sort of hospital garment, but of course she was wearing the same clothes she had left the house in that morning, with the same hair and make up, and the same bright eyes. She didn't look like the inmate of an institution at all.

"Bloody hell," she said, sitting heavily on the bench beside us. "I'm gasping for a fag." She was already lighting one. "They've got some right nutters in here. There's one woman keeps screaming and clinging to the walls."

She took a long drag on her cigarette, and we waited. There was a clear sense that we were her audience, waiting to hear her story.

"Well, then," she said. "This has been a bugger of a day, hasn't it? That bastard Warren - it was *him* that was harassing *me*. He's a complete nutcase. You remember what he was like, don't you, Amy, when we were back in New Gaia? We left there to get away from him. Volatile, he is, probably bipolar. It's him they should have arrested, not me. Bastard."

She paused, flicking ash. "Anyway." She flashed us a wry look. "Do you like my ruse? Getting them to bring me here? They would have charged me, you know; it was serious police stuff, they arrested me and everything. Threats to kill, they called it, and possession of an offensive weapon - how bad does that sound? So, I did a bit of wailing, some beautiful histrionics, and I told them I didn't know what I was doing, and they brought me here, and handed me over to the shrinks."

She grinned, and took another drag from her cigarette. "I reckon a couple of nights in here and the police will leave me alone altogether."

130

"Are you alright, then?" said Mark. "I mean..."

"Of course I'm alright, you daft git," she hissed. She looked over at the door and then back at us. "Oh, I've led them a dance: I told them all about the divorce, the fire, living in a caravan... they all feel sorry for poor me! I told them about Warren trying to get me to live in the woods with him with no running water, all that bollocks. I don't know why I let that bastard get under my skin... he certainly won't hear from me ever again, not after this, calling the bloody police on me, bastard." She scowled.

"Well, as long as you're alright," said Mark, tentatively.

"Oh, yeah, I'll be home in a few days." Another patient had appeared in the doorway, fumbling with a cigarette. "See her?" My mother was whispering now. "Her, there, she tried to top herself. Total nutcase."

I had always known that my mother had secrets, but I had never realised that she kept them from me. Although she had been curling up at Mark's fireside, she had also been out hunting down Warren. She lived lives within lives. She had pursued Warren and teased at him and flirted with him and fought passionately with him, all the while coming back to Mark's house as if there was nothing amiss; and eventually she had become obsessed and obsessive, like a ferret squirming deeper and deeper into a rabbit hole, looking for a fight.

When I went to bed that night, thinking of her in Acorn Ward, my life had changed, but not in the way I had expected six hours earlier, when Mark and I drove to the hospital. Nothing had changed for my mother: this was just another misadventure, another complication in a life of complications. She was home within two days, forgiven by the police; she cried on Mark's shoulder and confessed how silly she had been, how she had allowed Warren to draw her in, and she told Mark over and over that he was her rock and she was lucky to have him, that he was one in a million and she would never go off the rails again. But for me, something had changed, beneath the surface: my mother had secrets from me, and I began to reassess my history, reconsidering my memories as if I had suddenly discovered that these bland documents contained a hidden message in code. But the message, if it was there, was unreadable: it was not a message for me, and it remained unreadable. At New Gaia there had been obtuse remarks and obscure references in her fights with Warren, in Willow House and even Lucas Street there were funny looks, friends, phone calls... how did she fill her days when I was at school?

When we lived in Willow House, we slept in the same bed and lived our lives in the same room: her underwear, her letters, her lipsticks were spread out alongside mine; but now I understood that her mind was always closed to me, always secret. I was truly alone.

There was a breeze from the window now, and I was sitting gazing at the square of monochrome sky when the nurses came in to wash my mother.

"How are we today, Amelia?" The big nurse raised her voice cheerfully, as if my mother was only deaf, and shook out her plastic apron with a smile. "Lovely day, isn't it? Almost too warm. But we mustn't complain!" I had wriggled in my seat when they came in, as if I had been caught daydreaming when I should have been concentrating, and now I stood up to leave. The nurse smiled at me. "And how are we doing today?"

"Oh, I'm fine, thanks."

"That's good, that's good." They were moving around the bed professionally, tweaking and swishing and unfolding. The second nurse put down a roll of mottled pink fabric, which fell open to reveal itself as an old nylon nightdress. The big nurse looked at it distastefully.

"You know," she said, addressing me just as I was slipping out of the door. "You could bring your mum some of her own nightclothes from home." She was speaking carefully and deliberately, without meeting my eyes. "Might be nice for her to wear her own things."

I had got it wrong again. Of course, a proper daughter would bring nighties and pillows from home, perfumes perhaps, and soaps and personal things. A proper daughter would probably wash her own mother, sponging her tenderly instead of leaving her to strangers with plastic gloves and plastic aprons.

"Um..." It hit me that there was a good reason why I couldn't bring in her own things. "I don't actually have a key to her place."

132

Not only did I not have a key, I had never even been to her home; I had only an address for Christmas cards, written on a scrap of paper pinned to my fridge with a magnetic butterfly. It would be too embarrassing to explain; these nice nurses thought I was a nice normal daughter who popped round to her mum's for coffee, petted the cat and helped to change the lightbulbs.

"Oh goodness!" exclaimed the nurse. "Haven't you been given her belongings? Oh, I am sorry, I thought that had been done or I would have said something sooner... her handbag, it should have been signed over to you." She put everything down on the end of the bed, stripping off her clinging gloves, and said briskly: "Come on. We can sort this out right now."

I followed her along the corridors and she tracked down a nervous woman in a tweed suit, who produced paperwork for me to sign in exchange for my mother's handbag. There was also her jewellery in a lumpy brown envelope, and her clothes in a thin white bin liner. I realised that the hospital must have a whole store room, like a lost property office, for the handbags and false teeth and shoes of people snatched from their ordinary lives and interned in the wards.

Her handbag. When the nurses had finally gone, leaving my mother freshly washed and changed and rearranged, I sat with her handbag in my lap, feeling like a thief. I had no right to look in her handbag, no licence to go through her things. It felt furtive, and even a little sordid. I was an impostor, masquerading as a loved one; an enemy. My mother had been delivered into the hands of her enemy.

Now I would rummage in her bag, take possession of her keys, let myself into her home and poke around in her drawers, seeing all her things and pulling out her clothes. She was defenceless.

I sat with the weight of the bag in my lap and my hands on the soft worn leather. It was a floppy bucket bag, with a long shoulder strap and a narrow zip, like close-pressed lips. I slowly slid open the zip, from end to end. It was a short zip, and when the bag gaped it had only a small mouth, protecting the dark depths inside. I had a sudden memory of my mother from years before, complaining about the handbag she owned then - "This useless bloody bag!" she

133

grumbled, amiably. We were in Mark's kitchen. "The opening's too small to get my purse in and out." She had her hand inside, twisting the purse to get it out of the narrow gap, catching her hand on the tiny teeth of the zip. "Let go, Fido!" And we both laughed, because the bag was just like a dog, refusing to release the purse from its sharp little jaws.

The bag in my lap was like a lucky dip, the objects inside bumping against one another in the bottom. I put my hand in and came first to a tissue, a dry, scrunched-up tissue that had been there a while. I felt around. A purse: a large, stiff purse in black leather, zipped and poppered, which I set to one side. A phone: I pulled out her phone, slim and smooth, and hesitated. If I switched it on, I would be opening a cascade of information and people. I put the phone down.

The next thing I found was a diary. It was a small, fat diary, a day to a page, lined for tiny handwriting. I sat, holding it in my hand. Another cascade. But it didn't look as if it had been used, so I tentatively opened it at a random page, which was blank, and then flicked through a tumble of empty pages with a sense of relief. I didn't want to read a diary. The flow of white was suddenly interrupted by a burst of writing and I stopped and turned back: for about a dozen pages, in April, she had written something every day, in harsh black biro. Cornflakes 115, beans 162, 4 crackers 108. She must have been on a diet. The list of calories under each date seemed intense and obsessive, and it stopped as abruptly as it had begun, on 19th April. About two months ago.

There was a tube of lip balm, scuffed and dusty as if the bag had been its home for a long time, and a cheap biro with a crack along the length of its clear plastic body, and finally the keys. There were two keys: a slim ridged Yale and a fat, brassy mortice key, nipping the lining of the bag as I pulled them out. They were attached to a key ring with a red plastic tag, of the kind that suggested a low grade rental agency. I held the keys in my hand and I had no excuse for not going to her place.

I knew that her address was 2a Tennyson Street. It sounded like a small flat, or even a bedsit. I had pictured a two-ring cooker, a wooden-armed chair, and a window overlooking bins. I suppose I had assumed that her life had shrivelled up without me, that she had gradually got older and slower and poorer, and more unbalanced, maybe more frightening. She must live alone: if she had a boyfriend, he would surely be here. Unless he didn't know; I suddenly realised that I had a duty as next of kin to notify her friends and neighbours, to check her flat, to water her plants... what if she had a pet?

I knew nothing about her life now. I hadn't even thought about it. I had no idea what I would find at 2a Tennyson Street. Maybe she lived a shrunken life, in a single room bounded by a windowsill and skirting boards, pinned down by daytime television. Maybe she lived a chaotic life, sleeping all morning among empty bottles and dirty plates and alcoholic friends. Maybe she had an ordinary life, in a nice little flat, cleaning her teeth, answering the phone, cooking beans on toast.

Maybe I would learn nothing from 2a Tennyson Street; maybe she had a boyfriend or two and her real life was elsewhere, and I would find a sparse flat, empty of clues, as neat and musty as a dress at the back of a wardrobe. Maybe I would find an unused kitchen, a cold television and a sofa with cushions arranged like people for a photograph. Maybe she still had secrets and schemes, lives within lives, other places that I would never find.

Who was she now?

Maybe she had lots of friends and lovers, who had been wondering where she was; perhaps her phone was full of messages and I would find notes pushed under her door. Perhaps I would have to tell everyone, and they would come crowding to the ward with flowers and concern, demanding that the doctors save her, looking at me suspiciously and talking together in the corridor outside.

Perhaps I had just assumed she was alone, because I was alone myself.

I set off from the hospital to 2a Tennyson Street at seven o'clock that evening. I used my phone for directions, setting it down on the passenger seat like a friend. I was so nervous that my hands were sweating and slippery on the steering wheel. It helped to pretend I was a solicitor or a social worker making a professional

135

visit to the address of a client. This was a practical mission, after all: I was just going to a flat to pick up some clothing.

The warm weather had lured everyone out into the streets, and there were children on bicycles and people in summer clothes, laughing, and unexpected tables outside some of the bars in the city centre. It didn't feel as late as seven. Tennyson Street was part of a grid of Victorian terraces behind the railway station. A lot of the houses had been turned into stacks of bedsits, and there were small businesses nestled among them: a minicab firm, a vape shop and a tattoo parlour. I turned slowly into Tennyson Street, but the house numbers, when I eventually detected them, started at 76, so I guessed 2a was at the other end. There were cars parked on both sides of the road and not much room down the middle; I encountered a van coming briskly towards me and I had to back up and skew off into a space so he could get past. I could hear an ice cream van in the near distance, playing an aggressively frantic jingle. A woman in a vest top rattled by with a pushchair, shouting to a toddler.

I could see roughly which building was number 2, but there was nowhere to park outside, so I turned the corner into the next road, and saw that it was blocked off at the end by the wall that ran alongside the canal. Parked cars were jammed in all around me and I couldn't see a way to turn around. I felt hot and claustrophobic, in a clumsy car; I felt as if people would come out and stare at me and somehow know I was a terrible daughter. I had to reverse back past the end of Tennyson Street and into a space that I found, gratefully, outside some smaller houses and a derelict church.

I would have to walk back round the corner to 2a Tennyson Street. I was holding my mother's keys in my hand and I expected to be challenged in some way: I felt sure someone would come out of one of the other flats and ask who I was, but so far there seemed to be no-one around. There was a smell from a Chinese takeaway, perhaps in the next street, and I felt suddenly hungry. The building had a front door directly onto the street and five buzzers labelled simply with the letters a to e, but the front door was unlocked and actually ajar.

I pushed in to a hallway that was dark and unfurnished. There was junk mail on the floorboards. The stairs took off suddenly on the left and on the right there were two doors: one at the front of the house wearing the letter b, and one at the back stuck with the letter a.

I was still sweating and I felt a bit sick: empty, hungry and nervous. It was quiet. The key in the mortice lock rolled over with a smooth clunk but the Yale was old and worn and the key was unwilling in the slim lock. After some jiggling it turned, and the door opened, but I had to stand there jiggling some more to get the key to come back out of the slot. I still expected someone to come flying out of the other flat, but the whole house stayed silent. The uncarpeted hallway sounded hollow.

I stepped into the flat and let the door click shut behind me. There was a strange, undefinable smell. There seemed to be just one room; perhaps there was a shared bathroom upstairs. Instead of a curtain there was a white sheet draped over the curtain rail, glowing with evening sunlight, creating the atmosphere of a stuffy tent. The room itself remained dim, like the room of an invalid.

It was a bedsit: a scrappy, impersonal room put together by a hasty landlord. There was a single bed, messy with clothes, standing high on castors, and underneath it I could see fluffy dust, tissues and dog-eared magazines. There was a torn armchair, with a jumper curled up on the seat like a cat, and balanced on the arm a full ashtray and a mug with a pale disc of coffee in the bottom. There was a brown stain on the wall where there had once been a gas fire; the pipe and tap stuck up out of the floor. There was a burnt patch on the carpet, black and coarse, and the coil of an energy saving lightbulb hung unshaded in the centre of the room.

Against the wall there was a kitchen cupboard unit and a stainless steel sink, and a very old gas cooker, white but flecked with black where it had been chipped. Above, the wall had been pinned with posters. I stood and read them. The first showed a picture of a tree, and the writing said 'Sometimes you have to stop thinking so much and just go where your heart takes you'. The next depicted an open pink envelope and over it was printed 'If you carry one thing with you today, let it be this: you are smart, you are beautiful, and you are strong'. The next in line was a dusty road and the words 'No matter how far you have travelled in the wrong direction, you can always turn around'. Finally there was a big yellow sun and 'You attract the energy you give off. Listen to your soul. Think positively. 'The word positively had been underscored several times in biro.

The sink was crowded: a sticky bottle of gloopy green washing up liquid, a dribbling bottle of shampoo, a matted washing up brush, a squashed toothpaste tube and a toothbrush whose handle was caked with dry white paste. Alongside, on the formica top of the kitchen cupboard, there was a jar of instant coffee, a stained teaspoon, a kettle, a tin opener, some nail scissors, a little pile of pound coins, a roll of toilet paper, a box of paracetamol, a screwdriver with a black and yellow handle, and an unfolded letter. The letter had been opened out, but its confinement in an envelope and left it creased into severe thirds. I saw an official heading and stepped nearer. I could read it without touching it. At the top there was a purple logo and the words National Probation Service. 'Dear Ms Nash, 'the letter read. 'It has come to my attention that you have missed an appointment with your Community Mental Health Nurse. I must remind you that it is a condition of your Community Sentence that you must keep in regular contact with her and co-operate with her in every way. If you are having transport difficulties, please contact me... 'The words 'Fuck off 'had been written in biro, in sharp capitals, across the bottom of the letter.

There was a chest of drawers beside the bed, the drawers sticking out because they were too stuffed to close. I didn't want to touch them but I had to complete my mission. I was hurrying now, wanting to get away from this awful room, so I jerked open the top drawer as far as it would go and pulled out clothes: socks, pants, t-shirts. There was nothing that looked like nightwear, but she probably didn't have any. I uncrumpled a few of the t-shirts, choosing the two biggest and dropping the others on the bed. The drawers had a smell to them and it had infected the clothes; it was a smell of old wood and dozens of lives. I bundled the t-shirts around two pairs of pants and left, locking the mortice behind me.

I realised that I had been hoping to find a neat and happy life. I had been hoping to find friends and lovers, pets and houseplants: signs that my mother was living a vivacious and breezy life, a normal life with lunch dates and photographs in frames. Because if she had slid into a degenerate and desperate life, it was because of me, it was me that had propelled her that way. It was my fault.

It had been a very long day. The insistent sun was finally setting, and my windows were lit with a violent display of pink and orange. I sat on my sofa watching the small but lurid patch of sky, eating crackers straight out of the packet.

I realised, now, that I had never really left the past behind; never really left my mother behind. Our estrangement was in itself a connection. Hostility is as powerful as love, just as intense and inescapable. There had always been a bond between us, the immutable bond between mother and child, and in spite of secrets, differences and betrayals we were always family. I was her next of kin and she was mine. She was like a part of my body, and I was a part of hers.

Maybe I even saw myself in her flat, in my own alternative existence, or future, as a lonely middle aged woman. Part of me was her, part of her was me.

It was like an understanding, a knowledge of each other; the very essence of family. Everyone else is, and will always be, a stranger. We had hated one another but we could never deny each other; we could walk away from one another but the other would always be there. This was the true meaning of next of kin: we were born of the same past, grown in the same patch of soil, with the same view of the world, the exact view that no-one else would ever see. All those years that we had been together were known only to us.

"You're my child," she said to me on the day we left New Gaia, and she walked out on Warren. "You're my child; I made you. I could never love anyone else as much as I love you."

Friday

It was another hot day. In my anxiety to dress appropriately, I avoided shorts and ended up in a long floaty skirt that I had once bought when I thought I might like to be the kind of person who wore long floaty skirts; by the time I parked at the hospital I was feeling vaguely as if I was in disguise. There was too much fabric, piled up in my lap when I sat in the car and swirling round my legs as I climbed out. I had to be careful not to trap some of it in the door. Even my shoes looked nonplussed.

Swishing across the car park in the sun, I remembered that my mother's window was overlooking me, and I stopped, squinting up, to try to identify which window in the building above me was hers. There were actually hospital buildings on two sides of the car park, but I knew which was hers from the angle of the view when I had looked out the day before; it was a large, modern, sand-coloured block dimpled with small dark windows. My mother's room would be on the first floor. I was surprised to see that there were two further floors above, a huge part of the hospital that was unknown to me, since I hadn't even realised that the stairs continued up beyond my mother's ward. The inside and the outside of the building were hard to put together in my mind. There were eight windows on the first floor, and I tried to visualise the layout of the ward and match the windows to rooms, deciding eventually, with reasonable certainty, that her window was the third from the right.

I remembered that a college friend had once sent me a postcard from a holiday in Spain; it bore a picture of a giant, shiny hotel and my friend had drawn a smiley face on one of the balconies to indicate which was hers. It was exciting, identifying her room in that huge grid of identical white balconies and identical black windows, almost as if I could see her there, tiny and real, waving at me. It was just as gratifying, now, identifying my mother's window. It was a familiar space in this enormous, convoluted building, and in identifying the window I was projecting myself inside. The room had become one of the spaces of my life, like my home or car or workplace, a place where I belonged, a place I could walk to without noticing the way, and walk into without announcing myself, and sit down in without self-consciousness. From the car park, I could look up at that window and know where I was going, already connected with the room inside.

Beyond the sliding doors I had to slip through a little group of older people, smiling and chatting as if they were on a day out. The sunny weather had made everyone slow down and relax. A porter was leaning on an empty wheelchair and the woman at the information desk was gesturing extravagantly as she gave an elderly couple directions. The kiosk ladies were busily opening up and a nurse caught a door as it was closing to call something humorous to a friend. I walked along the coloured lines and wondered at the configuration of the building, the perpendicular corridors and sudden stairwells and flapping swing doors. It was an adaptive building, eager to function, but formed without planning, like something built by wasps or rabbits; it had been formed by additions and alterations, by meetings and paperwork, memos and applications.

Here was my mother's room, and the window I had seen from below. My chair had been moved slightly, perhaps by cleaners, and I tugged it back into position and sat down, arranging my excessive skirt.

Her eyes were slightly open today, and she had been raised at the head and shoulders, her arms at her sides pinning down the sheets. The morphine dispenser throbbed slowly. I got up to open the window and sat down again. People passed rhythmically in the corridor: a trolley wheel squeaking, footsteps steady, voices even.

I was remembering my last meeting with my mother, in that café, when she wore a green leather coat and fidgeted with a forbidden cigarette. She ate half of a tuna sandwich and added a paper tube of sugar to her coffee more than once. I didn't think, at the time, about how or where she was living, but now I had seen her current home in Tennyson Street, I realised that she had

141

probably come out to meet me that day from a bedsit, hostel or halfway house with black mould and fetid carpets. She had got ready to see me in a seedy bathroom, applying her makeup in a dirty mirror that wasn't her own. I felt a retrospective sympathy for her, but she had been dangerous that day. Tigers were once hunted as fearsome beasts; now they are protected as vulnerable creatures, but they still have claws and teeth.

"I suppose you're alright for money?" she said, in response to me paying when the waitress brought the bill. "Yes, he saved it all for you, didn't he?" The words "you're" and "you" were jabbed at me with a twist to her mouth and a thrusted chin; she looked at me spitefully. I ignored her and counted money from my purse, but I could feel her glowering, just as if she was giving off heat.

Earlier, she had said: "What are we doing here, anyway?" It was as if the words had formed in her mind as an attack, but when they reached her lips they lost confidence and fell from her mouth almost in bewilderment; she looked suddenly tired. I responded, though, to the original intent, and rolled my eyes theatrically.

"I suppose," I said, "I suppose I thought we ought to keep in touch, you know, since we are related, much as you obviously hate me..." Someone at the next table looked round sharply and I had to lower my voice. "Anyway, you rang me."

"Did I?" She still looked tired.

"Don't you remember?"

Her eyes suddenly woke up. "What do you mean by that?" she asked, savagely. "Do you still think I'm a nutcase? Of course you do, sitting there all Little Miss Proper, sitting in judgement on me..." People were looking at us again. "Do you think I came here from the nuthouse? In a white van?"

"Don't be silly." This time it was me who sounded weary. The whole conversation followed this pattern: a series of impetuous wild thrusts that neither of us had the inclination to follow through. Everything had been said before. There were no vulnerable spots left, nowhere a new wound could be inflicted. We were sparring in full armour, impregnable but exhaustingly heavy. We stepped down and fell instead to agreeing that the tuna sandwiches were dry and the salad scrawny.

142

I can't remember our last words to one another. We got up, moved our chairs and looked to the door. I put on my coat. Standing, I became more aware of the other customers and their awareness of us; I think I blushed, and resented my mother for her perennial public displays. I must have said goodbye.

I sent her a card at Christmas, but I didn't receive one from her. I had more than a dozen cards from people at work and they cluttered my windowsills and mantelpiece, occasionally falling like butterflies in a draught. I assumed she was either snubbing me or just hadn't got round to it in time; she had never been an efficient person and birthday cards were always late. I didn't think much about it at all.

She didn't call me again, and I didn't call her.

Mark had old friends, most of whom were couples; sometimes he and my mother were invited along to pub quizzes or informal parties. My mother was suspicious of slotting into the gap in a long-established seating plan; she was scornful of their "get togethers" and self-conscious chumminess, the hugs, reminiscences and nicknames. I got to know their names from her slanted comments: "I suppose Davey will enthral us with one of his stories again," she would say, as Mark helped her into her coat, "I wonder which one he'll repeat tonight?" Jenny, I learnt, was constantly boasting about her genius six-year-old, whilst Susie never stopped telling everyone how sweet they were and how much she loved them all. Sometimes my mother was drunk when they came home, and sometimes things had been said. "I don't care what that bitch thinks," she would be saying in the hall, as Mark shut the door carefully and wiped his feet on the mat, "I'll say what I bloody well like."

Mark was conciliatory. "I don't think she meant to upset you."

"I'm not upset! Do you think a silly bitch like that can upset me? I don't give a crap about her and her perfect bloody family." I was upstairs, and I could hear them move into the kitchen, where my mother continued to expound angrily against the rising note of the kettle. Another evening she had a full blown row with one of Mark's friends, and was furious when, several days later, she ascertained that he had telephoned to apologise on her behalf.

143

"I'm not your dead fucking wife so don't try to turn me into her..." The fight was protracted and vigorous. We were driven to walk out on Mark; she threw some of our clothes randomly into a suitcase and brought us back to the caravan park in a taxi that smelled of honeysuckle air freshener. I felt sick. The caravan was damp; taken by surprise, it was like a host in a dressing gown, unprepared for guests. My mum slammed around the kitchen and made black coffee. I put the television on and sat staring at it, hoping that, unobserved, the room would warm up around me and re-form into its familiar self.

Mark came that night and there was crying. In the end we went back with him in his car.

My mother's own friendships flared and died without ever really taking hold. Sometimes she would light on a happy routine of meeting Anita for coffee or dropping in to see Cathy, but after a while she would find Anita irritating or take offence at Cathy's obsession with cats. She was impatient and dissatisfied with other people. For a while she had a friend called Belinda, an uncompromising woman with a sheet of shiny blond hair who wanted to be an actress. When I came home from school she would be on the settee with her feet curled under her, sipping peppermint tea. My mother picked up her habit of calling everyone 'poppet'. Sometimes they had a "girls 'night", with wine in goblets and spicy crisps in bowls, and Mark would have to go out to the pub. Eventually, though, Belinda became a disappointment. "That woman's an emotional vampire," my mother said. "She was bloody maudlin last night, weeping." Belinda faded out of my mother's life and we stopped buying peppermint tea.

She was much the same with jobs. She started work at a little clothes shop that she called a 'boutique', and for a time she loved the owner, Harriet, and brought home jackets bought with a twenty per cent discount; but Harriet became overbearing and bossy and my mother walked out. She worked at a bar in town and started wearing black clothes and eyeliner, but the bar manager turned out to be an idiot kid who thought he knew more than she did, and the hours were outrageous. She took a job on a hotel reception desk and came home gorged with stories of eccentric businessmen and indolent cleaners, but the stories dried up and the work became drudgery; worse, the hotel decided to introduce uniforms for receptionists, so she handed in her notice. She would never do a job that came with a uniform.

"I couldn't bear a job-for-life," she used to say. Her father had been a "lifer". Every day for forty-two years he worked in the same building - "Can you imagine?" she said. "I'd rather be dead." She had rejected her parents long ago, and moved four hundred miles to escape. Her siblings all had boring jobs and boring marriages and boring children and boring houses.

"I suppose that makes me the weirdo," she said. It was her birthday, and the three of us were sitting round Mark's kitchen table encircling lasagne, wine and candles. Mark shook his head.

"No, not at all," he said. "You just didn't fit your family. It happens." He grinned. "You were just too exciting for them."

My mother laughed and looked warmly across the candles at Mark. "Anyway," she said. "You're my family now."

"That's right."

Later in the morning, the nurses stopped by to shift her into a different position, re-assembling the sheets and plumping the pillows very professionally. The big nurse gave me a tender smile.

"Glad to see you've opened the window," she said, nodding towards it. "Another lovely day! Beautiful." She and the other nurse took hold of my mother in the crooks of their elbows and heaved her after one-two-three, like the indulgent friends of a drunk. "There we go, that's much better." The nurse ripped a moisture stick from its wrapper and wiped it around the inside of my mother's lips, and then checked her position and examined the morphine machine. "Lovely," she said. Crumpling the used stick in its wrapper, she gave me another smile and then the two nurses left.

In her new position, her eyelids had drooped, and she looked like someone who was falling asleep, but caught and frozen in the moment, her eyes not completely closing. It reminded me that she was caught: caught between living and dying, neither one nor the other. It reminded me, too, of seeing her fall asleep on the sofa one night: she and Mark had come home late, quite drunk and giddy,

145

and I had come downstairs in my slippers, because I was still awake. Mark made mugs of tea. There was a documentary on television about some old band from the sixties, a mix of distorted footage and interviews with bearded old men sitting in front of framed discs or guitar collections. My mother hadn't spoken for a while and when I looked back she had fallen asleep, head thrown back, mouth open, arms flopped at her sides with the palms up, like someone crying out to the sky. My eyes met Mark's and we both grinned. The room was peaceful and there was the same sense of relief as when a crying baby finally settles.

Here, though, in this hospital bed, she wasn't falling asleep, but draining away.

I hadn't spoken to her for a couple of days, so when I did my voice surprised me.

"Hello, Mum."

I paused.

"I brought a few things in for you."

I couldn't bring myself to say I'd been in her flat, even though I knew she would not, could not, respond. If there was the outside chance of an outside chance that she could hear me, a tiny possibility that there was still something of her mind in there that could hear me and understand what I said, then I didn't want to say that I had been in her flat. She would be horrified - I had taken advantage while she lay here, helpless, and now I knew about her, more than she would ever had wanted me to know. More than I wanted to know. If I told her, if I spoke aloud of her flat, it would be like a committee that had already come to a decision receiving new information. It would open up so many new questions, and re-evaluations, and emotions: perhaps humiliation for her, guilt for me; perhaps vindication for one of us, or neither of us; perhaps regret - but it was too late, too late now for any new evidence, too late for any new discussion. It was too late to change anything.

"I opened the window," I said. "It's another hot day." I suddenly wondered why I was talking, and stopped.

Mark's kitchen was lit by spotlights in the ceiling, and in the evenings the light glinted off stainless steel and golden bottles of olive oil, casting patches of angular darkness about the room.

146

Sitting at the table, I had two shadows, created by two separated spotlights; they moved together but at subtly different heights, overlapping. One evening my mother came in and slammed her handbag down on the table. She took out a cigarette and lit it rebelliously.

"We saved some for you," said Mark, steadily, not taking his hands out of the sink or turning to meet her eyes.

She blew smoke and irritably picked a flake of tobacco from her lip. "Don't you want to know where I've been?"

She had brought a smell of alcohol into the room with her. Mark looked round furtively and then directed himself back to the sink. His shirt sleeves were rumpled back and his wrists disappeared into white apple-scented froth.

"Aren't you going to ask?"

"Well." Mark took a breath. He seemed to be stalling for time, as if he were the one who had to explain himself.

"Don't you care?"

At times like this, my mother was too large for the room she was in, like a clumsy child or an excitable pet that had to be steered away from breakables. Mark looked doggedly at the lumpy suds in the sink, still committed to the belief that he could calm her down by being calm himself. "Look," he said. "Look, you don't have to - "

"Oh, for fuck's sake, you're so pathetic." She snatched up her bag. "I don't know why I bothered coming home at all."

At times like these my mother was a gathering storm, or even a tornado, sucking up everything around her and drawing it in to her swirl. It was inevitable that she would again lift us and our belongings from Mark's and pitch us back to the caravan site; it was as if she couldn't stop herself. She was carried by her own momentum.

"I suppose you think I'm drinking too much," she said to me, viciously, one night, when I sat eating baked beans in the smoke-filled caravan. She didn't want food, only wine and cigarettes. Her make-up clogged her eyes and she alternated between anger and self-indulgent depression. We had fights, both of us slamming the cardboard-thin doors, and I think she enjoyed them. It felt at times

147

as if we were following a script. When we went penitently back to Mark, everything was blamed on alcohol, and for a while she wore her face pale and preoccupied and behaved like an invalid. Mark cared for her.

During that summer Mark took us for a day at the seaside. It was a long drive and the ant-like column of traffic knotted up at village roundabouts, but Mark kept us cheerful and the sky stayed blue. We were all three quite giddy on the promenade, eating pink candy floss that melted to grit in my mouth, and a stick of mint-flavoured rock that Mark shattered into mouth-sized pieces against a wall. We ate fish and chips in a mirrored cafe and spent the whole afternoon in amusement arcades: the penny falls machines were mesmerising and I can still remember watching each ten pence coin that I rolled into the slot glide down a convoluted series of inclines and crash onto the uneven pile of silver, the whole bank of them moving steadily to and fro; I remember the agonised anticipation as an overhanging clump wobbled but did not fall, and the elation when a small collapse sent a noisy cascade down the chute to the tray at my knees.

We said we would go back another day, but every Saturday there was a problem: Mark's car broke down, or he had to work, or my mum had to work, or Mark was painting a friend's garage, or it was raining; Mark said we should go even if it was raining, but my mum pulled a face at that. We never made it to the seaside again.

Lunchtime. There was already a queue at the hospital cafeteria, and it was too warm, the blue sky trapped behind large windows that couldn't be opened. I shuffled my tray and looked at the burnt cottage pie and roasted vegetable tarts, brown and speckled with cubes of grey courgette. I chose a thin celeriac soup and a crisp white bread roll. The crust shattered and sprayed powdery crumbs when I broke it.

There were four people sitting at the table alongside mine, and one of them was a man with a loud voice. I couldn't hear the other contributors to the conversation, but his voice rang out clearly, so it sounded as if he was declaring, at intervals, a series of insistent non-sequiturs. "Yes, yes, well, I said that, I said that." "I don't think it's that far actually." "Of course it was back in March, well, no, perhaps it was April, no, March, I'm sure it was March. March." I let the sound of my own munching fill my head to drown him out, and I thought vaguely about work. Friday was the last proper day of the week, apart from the emergency court on Saturday morning to accommodate Friday night arrests. Friday morning court was mainly for road traffic cases, generally heard in the absence of any defendants, who could write in with their guilty pleas and be informed of their fines by post; it made for a relaxed court, more like a casual meeting than a ceremonial performance. Sometimes it was interrupted by someone brought into custody for breaching bail conditions, and the magistrates would have to straighten up and put on their sombre faces ready for the custodians to bring the accused up from the cells.

I wondered which day would be cut from my week.

The man at the next table was still speaking loudly, his voice intruding into my head, pushing aside my thoughts. "He'll arrive the day before, I don't know when, I don't know when, at some time, he'll get there." A pause whilst someone else spoke quietly and then: "Yes, I know, you don't know when, you can't be sure, no, you can't be sure." Although I could hear every word he said, there was no narrative without the other voices, so it was like white noise, or static, distracting me. I finished my cup of tea. "Some of these places, you know, some of these places, they'll tell you in advance..."

His repetition of phrases enhanced the intrusiveness of his voice. He spoke slowly, very clearly, unavoidably. It's terrible how easily you can lose yourself when your thoughts are scattered by encroachment from the external world. As I finished my tea, it was as if I didn't exist any more. I had been invaded.

"Well, I said, I said, it's a good job he does know where he's going, because they're no help at all." "Yes, I know, that's what he said, that's what he said to me, too." I realised, listening to him repeating himself, that it was more than a tic; it was an attempt to keep hold of the thread of the conversation, a safety rope while he struggled from one assertion to another. As I tried not to listen, it felt as if he was using my head as an anchor. "No, he didn't say that

149

to me, he didn't say that to me, you see..." I set down my empty cup and left the table, retreating with relief into the blended voices and sounds of the corridor, a background mumble that allowed me to repossess my own mind.

Whenever we left Mark and went back to live in the caravan, I could no longer go home for lunch, because the journey from school to the caravan park was too far, necessitating a reliance on the frequent but capricious number 62 bus. I took instead to hiding in the school library at lunchtime. Along one wall was a row of stunted desks in cubbyholes, little isolated boxes where you could sit facing a blank wall, with wooden panels on either side screening off your neighbours. Most students preferred to use the computers or cluster around the open, friendly tables, so the cubicles were invariably empty, looking, as they did, like places of punishment. I, however, liked to sit with my back to the room; I made a nest of the desk with my notepads and pencil case and an open but unread copy of *To Kill A Mockingbird*. I wasn't studying but daydreaming, and doodling, and being alone and private.

In the classrooms where we had our lessons, the atmosphere was theatrical: there were confrontations and tears, stunts and laughter, secrets and giggling. Characters worked to outshine each other. Sometimes there was camaraderie and an outbreak of goodwill and allegiance, but just as often there was melodrama and treachery and a scramble to take sides. For a while I sat next to Chantelle in lessons, but she was anxious and unreliable, watching the other girls with frightened rabbit eyes as if she was trying to follow a book of manners written in a foreign language. She wore incredible make up, as carefully applied as calligraphy to fine paper: a perfectly smooth beige face with long black lashes and inked-in brows. We had nothing to say to one another, and eventually she found a nook to cling to in a popular group, although she still sought me out in Maths, so that she could look at my work when her own became too much. With Chantelle beside me as camouflage I could sit quietly while the other girls were performing, and as long as I displayed the correct responses of laughter, disbelief and horror at the appropriate moments I could achieve the appearance of vaguely fitting in.

One day we were allowed home early. There had been some sort of accident in the science lab, far more disappointing than initially rumoured but still serious enough for our double lesson to be cancelled and our science teacher to be required to clean up. The yawning, unfamiliar teacher who directed us into the hall and flicked on the lights told us desultorily to "do your homework or something" and then sat behind a pile of marking. It was clear that he wasn't counting us and didn't care if anyone came back from the toilet, or from fetching books, or if anyone wanted to wander off to use the computers or get to early football practice, so in a short time we were all whispering and shuffling, and about half of us had excused ourselves to go from the room and met up in a quiet corridor to plan a trip into town.

It was surprising that no other teachers appeared, because this was no silent sneaking out: there was giggling and even exclamations as we collected our coats from the cloakroom, pattered through the corridors, called to each other in stage whispers to stop running, clutched at one another in alarm and finally burst out of the building, leaving the door banging, and pounded across the playground, laughing.

From the playground we crossed the teachers 'car park and found ourselves in the street. Once there, all the others set off arm in arm for an adventure in town, and I slipped away, unnoticed, to set off in the other direction, for home.

The weather was restless that day, a squally wind snatching at litter and hair; as I walked it started to rain in bursts, and I hurried to the shelter of the bus stop with my head down, squinting when the rain splattered in my face. I was lucky: there was a bus already waiting, rumbling, held back by an old lady in a shapeless coat dismantling an umbrella. As the bus gently tossed me about, juddering and grinding through traffic, I looked forward to dry clothes, a cup of tea, chocolate biscuits and television.

From the bus stop I had to walk across the caravan site, and the wind slung gusts of rain at me as if I was walking along a seafront in a storm. My hair was dripping into my eyes and it was only when I opened the door of our caravan that I noticed the lights were on inside. I had expected Mum to be at work. I stood, gaping, until

Mum saw me and shouted "Fuck off!" She was on the settee having sex with a man I didn't know: there were arms and legs and clothes and panting, in a vaguely comical disorder. I had a moment when force of habit turned me towards my bedroom, but Mum shouted "Fuck off!" again so I stepped back out into the rain, clanging down the steps.

I didn't really know what to do, so I just walked, surrendering to a soaking. The sky had darkened and there were lights in the windows of most of the caravans. We had moved out of Mark's only five weeks before, and I had, I now realised, expected that we would go back. I was crying now, and furious with her. Why couldn't she just settle down with Mark and live like a normal person? Why did she have to ruin everything?

I didn't want to go home while her new man was still there, so I kept walking, out of the caravan site and along the main road, looking for somewhere to shelter. There was a row of rain-dark houses, a funeral director's, a vet's and another row of houses. The stream of cars all had their lights on, white in one direction, red in the other. There was a fish and chip shop that hadn't opened yet, and a dentist's with steamed-up windows. At last I came to a petrol station and wandered into the shop. The man behind the counter looked at me suspiciously but I turned my back and stood sightlessly in front of the display of magazines.

It could have been funny, walking in on her having sex, and one day it did become a funny, sensational story I told to my college friends. At the time, though, I was cold and wet, and the scene I had witnessed was animal and destructive. I stood in front of the magazines and cried.

My mother, too, turned it into a funny story. "There we were, at it hammer and tongs, and you walked in!" There was a manic edge to her in those days: she was a bit too bright, a bit too loud, sweating a little under thick makeup like a contestant on a talent show. She rushed at everything and never came to rest. One night she was out late and woke me in tears; I made her coffee while she sat beneath the harsh lightbulb in the cold caravan, blowing her nose through a crumbling tissue. She hadn't even unzipped her boots. "I guess I'm having a midlife crisis," she said. I put the coffee into her hand. "I don't know what's fucking wrong with me. I've got the perfect fucking man in love with me but I keep screwing it up."

When she and Mark got back together again, this time there was some sort of negotiated agreement to "take it slowly". My mother treated Mark like a programme of medication or rehabilitation: she took him in regular, measured doses. They arranged dates and she attended them. She talked about their relationship seriously and purposefully, as if Mark were something wholesome and therapeutic. He appeared at the door of our caravan and waited outside like a prom date, rocking on his heels, while she found her shoes and bag, said goodbye to me, and meekly followed him out to his car. They went out for meals in restaurants, to the cinema, for a drive in the country. He brought her home by midnight.

To me, it felt like a pretence, an elaborate game perpetrated on me like a joke: at that time, more than ever before, I yearned for the normality of life at Mark's house, breakfast in the kitchen, the cushions on the sofa and the angle of the TV, the way the light fell across my bedroom. The vivid and meticulous memories of Mark's house were not so much packed in my head as bursting out, lungeing at me when I sat on the bus or looked at my maths book: clear, insistent memories of a house so real and yet from which I was banished. I could smell the washing up liquid Mark used, hear the tick of the clock in the hall, feel the stair carpet under my socks. I badly wanted to live there again, but I was no more than a minor character in this play: my mother and Mark arranged their formal programme of events, and I wasn't even there to witness what was said.

I was applying to college to study A levels. My school didn't have a sixth form so my GCSE exams marked the end of my incarceration there. My mother suggested that I use Mark's address for my college application, rather then reveal that I lived on a caravan site. For a while I daydreamed that we would actually have to move into Mark's to authenticate my application form, and I even studied the more obscure links of the college website for references to home visits or electoral rolls, but I soon had to resign myself to using Mark's address as no more than a mail drop, and a mail drop that I didn't even visit myself. My college correspondence was brought by Mark when he came to pick up my mother.

Their relationship was still regulated by dates: a Friday night meal, Sunday lunch in a pub, perhaps a midweek trip to the cinema, and it felt like a kind of limbo, as if a ceasefire had been signed but no treaty agreed. Mark's mother, Barbara, avoided us politely, and there were no Sunday lunches in her caravan. Sometimes, when I walked home across the site after school, I could hear the parrot inside her thin walls, and it made me think of her warm living room and salty gravy. I was working for my GCSEs and I spent my evenings in my tiny room, lying on the bed amongst books and highlighter pens.

My college offer was relayed to me third hand: the letter was delivered to Mark's house, propped on his mantelpiece and then transferred to the glovebox of his car, handed over to my mother when they kissed goodbye and then carried into the caravan and left leaning against the kettle for me to discover in the morning. In the same way, reports of my mum's relationship with Mark were relayed to me like formal notifications from a distant campaign; occasionally she would come home irritated, or bored, or happy, but I could glean no overall sense of progress or retreat.

Eventually there was one evening when she came home earlier than expected. I was sitting in my bed with my knees up, writing an essay about the causes of the First World War. She came in to the doorway of my room and stood there, because there was nowhere in the room to sit, or even stand.

"That's it," she announced. "We're done. It's never going to work."

She left my doorway and went through to the sitting room, obviously expecting me to follow so she could tell me the whole story. I scrambled out of bed in my nightshirt, pulling on leggings that caught on my feet and a jumper that tugged my hair, and went to sit barefoot on the sofa while she boiled the kettle.

They had tried to make it work, she said, but it was like flogging a dead horse. She had had enough of wasting her time.

She was too old to waste time. She still had her coat on and she sat down heavily, smelling of outdoors and pubs. "Never fall in love with a widower," she said. "A divorcee is fine: they've been in love, they've fallen out of love, and they generally hate the person they've left behind. But a widower is still in love. She died, and he'll always love her. I feel like I'm his mistress." She lifted her coffee to her lips, but it was still too hot to drink.

"I'm sure you'll get over this," I said. "You and Mark keep splitting up but you always get back together."

She shook her head. "No, that's it, it's over. I'm not drunk, I'm not upset, just tired - tired of Mark. I don't know why I've been wasting my time."

"But you two are meant to be together."

She snorted. "Fairytale stuff. He's boring, he's staid. He's like someone's dad."

"Well, what kind of man do you want?"

"Oh, someone exciting, someone who makes me happy, someone unpredictable, fun, crazy..."

I was exasperated. "You're the one looking for a fairytale. Mark's not going to wait around for you forever, you know; you can't keep messing him about like this."

I sounded vicious, and she looked at me, surprised, and then angry.

"Don't try to tell me about relationships - you're just a silly little girl..."

We tumbled into a row, our voices rising until we both stood up, bouncing out of our seats, calling each other selfish, swearing. Of course, fighting in a caravan is like swimming in a bathtub, sploshing water over the side and knocking hips and elbows against slippery surfaces; there was no room for gesturing or throwing things and we were too close for shouting. We knew the whole site could hear us. I felt a violent urge to take hold of her, to push her or hit her, as we stood face to face in the tiny room; then it struck me that she might feel the same, and fear made me walk away, past her and into my room, banging the flimsy door and sitting firmly on the floor behind it, hugging my shins.

155

I heard her come up behind me. The door itself was so thin that her voice was as loud as it would be with nothing between us.

"You're a selfish little cow! You expect me to live my life around you, but get this: I'm not lumbering myself with him for the rest of my life just to give you a bloody father figure!"

We continued to shout abuse at each other through the walls, but in shorter and shorter bursts until the battle had gone cold and we each went to sleep scowling.

It was several weeks later when she casually said: "Mark rang. There's a letter for you at his place, a letter from the college." She was heating a tin of soup for our tea; I had just changed out of my school uniform. "He says he's in all day Saturday if you want to go over there and pick it up." She stirred the soup with a metal spoon, scraping a swirl around the pan and then clanging it on the rim. "I don't want to see him; you can go on your own."

So that Saturday I took a bus over to Mark's. It was sunny, a pretty day, and there were little children chalking in the street and falling off scooters. I still had a key to the door but I knocked and waited nervously. The children up the street were laughing and running. Although I hadn't been to the house for a long time, it seemed as familiar as if I had just left the day before. It was as if the house hadn't noticed I was missing; daily life was just bumbling along in that street as it always had done.

"Come on in!" Mark spread his arms in welcome, although his smile was sideways and shy. He was wearing his decorating clothes - faded, sagging jeans and a t-shirt irregularly patterned with smears and drips - and there was a transparent plastic sheet, like loose clingfilm, spread across the hall carpet. "I'm just painting the living room door," he explained. He was repainting it the same colour, white: it looked the same but shinier. There was a potent smell of gloss. "Go on through to the kitchen."

He hadn't re-arranged any furniture, but it somehow felt as if I was edging my way around obstacles and trying not to disturb anything. Mark, too, moved cautiously, perhaps because he had paint on his hands. "Cup of tea?" he said.

"Oh, no, no thanks," I said, automatically. To accept a cup of tea would be like accepting an embarrassingly lavish gift; besides, it would mean sitting down and talking and I didn't know what we would say.

"Looking forward to college?"

"Oh yes. I think so." It was a question I had been asked several times but I still didn't have a ready answer. The truth was that I was nervous and excited and confused and proud and shy and terrified and elated; but I understood that people who asked the question only wanted a polite yes.

I felt suddenly sad that Mark had become a person who only wanted a polite yes. Perhaps we had never been any closer than that. Perhaps no-one ever is any closer than that. I felt, wearily, that everyone I had ever known, apart from my mother, was a stranger, politely pretending to show an interest in me. I felt the strain of a world of strangers.

"Let me grab that letter for you." He went off into the living room, and I stood waiting in the kitchen. Again, the room felt as if I had never been away. There was a newspaper on the table and plates drying beside the sink, and a faint smell of a Saturday morning fry up. Mark came into the room with an envelope in his hand and passed it to me. "There you go."

"Thanks."

"It only came on Wednesday. I didn't think it would be urgent..."

"Oh, no, I'm sure it's not..."

"... or I would have dropped it round to you, of course."

"No, no, that's fine."

"Good."

"It won't be urgent."

"No."

"Probably just some general information, where to go on the first day, that sort of thing."

"Yes, probably."

"Yes."

"Exciting!"

"Yes!"

"Are you sure you don't want a cup of tea?"

"Oh, no thanks."

157

Our eyes wandered away from one another, and then wandered back.

"Anyway; I'd better go."

"Oh, okay."

I had the sudden thought that my bedroom was only just above me, and yet impossibly far away, as if a rift in space had opened up and split the galaxy in two. It was a room I had slept in, read in, thought in, been alone in night after night; a home; it was just up those stairs but I could never go back to it. It was yet another room sucked into the vacuum of my past.

"Thanks for letting me use your address." I waved the letter at him.

"No problem, any time. I mean, if you need to keep on using this address while you're at college, that's fine with me."

"Thanks." We stood smiling at each other as if we had just met. "Anyway." I turned and moved back along the hall, stepping carefully on the delicate plastic film. The smell of gloss paint saturated the house.

"You know," he said behind me, "you're welcome to drop in whenever you want. I mean, I know this was your home for a while; I mean, I don't want you to feel you can never come back. I mean, I know your mum and I... well, who knows, we've split up before. You never know what's round the corner. But what I'm saying is, whatever happens, you're always welcome here."

"Thanks." At the door I turned round to say goodbye.

Mark's kitchen is one of the places that I keep packed away in my memory. I can carefully take it out, unfold it and study it. I can feel the kitchen table under my forearms, see the sharp sunlight muffled by a blind on summer days, hear the sound of a cupboard opened and closed. The overhead spotlights on winter evenings, the furious fan in the oven, the occasional drip from the tap and Mark reflexively reminding us not to overtighten it. The red and blue stripes on the tea towels, the clatter of someone fumbling for a teaspoon in the cutlery drawer, the yelp of the toaster and the faint smell of toast just slightly overdone. I don't even have to close my eyes to remember; these perceptions are so powerful that they can crowd out the present world in front of me.

I have other places packed away, too: Bernard's polytunnel, shuddering in the wind, the dry smell of the stunted plants and the brittle shells of long dead snails stuck to the legs of his plastic chair; Tori's pottery studio, in an ancient, cold building infused with centuries of damp, the earthy smell of the clay and the wooden stool beneath me as cold as a stone, and Tori's boot moving up and down on the pedal of her wheel, producing a rhythmical mechanical sound that never changed. From time to time I take out these memories and run my hands over them, reciting them, deliberately remembering them so that they don't fade. I worry that perhaps, in the remembering, I distort them or touch them up - perhaps the very act or remembering, of re-memorising, actually degrades them, or alters them, like Chinese whispers. It's a risk I take. I suppose I'm afraid that if I left them packed away they might decay or wither without me knowing. Memories are so delicate.

In my mother's head the memories, packed away, are now lost, like chests aboard a sunken ship, lost forever at sea. All of it means nothing now. Memories are only for the living and they die with us. Her memories of me, of my father, of Willow House, of New Gaia, of Mark, of the caravan - all those carefully filed and fragile memories are washed away, soaked and illegible, gone.

I realised that when she was gone, most of my history would be mine alone. No-one else would remember reading magazines at Willow House, watching television from under a blanket at Golden Meadows, or the fire at Lucas Street. My only witness would be gone. My past was uncertified, uncorroborated, unverified. Packed away in my head, my memories were the only copies left.

I was solitary, more solitary than ever before. I felt old. I felt like an old woman telling a story that no longer mattered to anyone.

The nurses came again in the afternoon to wash her. I had been sunk deep in a swill of inconsequential thought and their arrival startled me; I had to scramble back into myself to sit up and smile at them.

"It's so warm!" exclaimed the big nurse. It was very warm, and the sky that filled the window was a soaring blue, like the seaside.

The nurses began to unpack and arrange their equipment and I stood up to go.

"How are we doing this afternoon?" the big nurse asked, kindly. "I hope you're looking after yourself."

"Oh yes," I said.

"That's good. Now off you pop for a coffee; we'll be fifteen minutes."

I went out of the ward but I didn't go for coffee; this time I found a stairwell with a big window and looked out. The handrail, of teak-coloured wood, cut across the window and I could lean on it at elbow height while I looked out. Instead of the car park, this window observed an odd patch of triangular tarmac and two big fenced-in tanks labelled 'oxygen'; there were profuse pipes and notices and it all looked grubby and industrial and yet oddly futuristic. Beyond, there was a high but flimsy wire fence holding back a patch of overgrown wasteland. To the side stood another module of the hospital, an old red brick building, perhaps Victorian, and a door that had no handle on the outside. Beside the door was a bright yellow plastic tub labelled 'Grit', for salting paths in winter.

The stairwell treated sound with a strange hollow effect: I would hear the swing door creak above or below me, and footsteps pattering, and voices reverberating slightly against the tall blank walls, getting louder as they came towards me, behind me where I stood facing the window; and then receding, until the other swing door squeaked and there was silence. Everyone was travelling from top to bottom or bottom to top, while I waited in the middle. I didn't turn around to look at anyone; the acoustics of the stairwell made footsteps and voices high and sibilant, so everyone sounded brisk and light. They were busy, moving quickly from top to bottom and from bottom to top like pulses of light, or messages, or maybe just a pattern, moving back and forth for no reason at all.

After a while the door of the Victorian building with no handle on the outside opened, and a man in overalls stepped out to smoke in the sun, holding the door open with his knee. He didn't look up at me, but I didn't feel alone any more, so I left the window and went back to see if they had finished with my mother.

160

Unlike my high school, which was one of those 1960s buildings that seem to have been put together from squares of blue and white plywood, my college was crafted from elegant grey stone. The doorways were tall and prefaced by broad, shallow steps; there were pillars and ridges and carved classical details. Inside there were high, frilly ceilings and wooden floors caked with old polish, and dimples up the centre of the staircase where the wood had been worn by generations of feet. Some of the windows could only be opened by a long pole, wielded by one of the braver teachers, unhooking a hinged panel at the top. It was the kind of place that made you want to carry a bundle of hardback textbooks self-importantly in front of your chest, or sit gazing dreamily upward in the cool of a morning, listening to a teacher's voice and chewing a pencil.

I studied History, Sociology and English, and although I quickly discovered a hatred for English it only encouraged me to enjoy the other two subjects all the more. The books we studied in English were archaic and excruciating; our eager teacher apparently expected us to seize on some coded meaning, but it was all a dull drone to me. It was like studying those pictures that suddenly reveal an image if you stare at them long enough. Shakespeare was a foreign language to me and I literally had to buy a translation, a book called *Easy Hamlet* which butchered the opaque poetry and rendered it into something absurdly modern and silly. Dickens and Bronte I could understand, but reading them was like trudging through deep, sticky mud for miles to get somewhere I didn't particularly want to go. In English lessons Elena and I took to pulling faces of comically outrageous incomprehension at each other, until it was hard not to giggle.

Opposite the college there was a McDonalds, and at lunchtime most of us would drift across to it in clumps. Having just left a weighty academic building, we could treat McDonalds as an ironic experience and revel in its trashiness. So many students spilled in at lunchtime that we had to be efficiently processed: first, we stood in thick queues, chatting and joking around, bubbling with laughter and occasional shouts, until we arrived suddenly at the till and had to snap to attention and remember what we intended to order, gawping at the bright pictures we had seen a hundred times before. The abrupt staff rattled out our orders, clattered down change and barked 'Can I help you please? 'over our shoulders to the next in line, fingers already poised above the till, while we moved to the next stage of processing: waiting at the side for our orders to be sizzled, flipped and packed. We were captive then, having paid, with no choice but to wait meekly. Finally we slipped into cold plastic benches, realising suddenly how little time we had left to eat before European History with Mr Walters.

In the winter we sat in our coats, hoods and scarves; as spring swept into summer it was too hot to sit against the windows and there was such competition for the outside tables that we would squash together or perch on the very edge of a bench. Some students sat on the college steps to drink coffee from cardboard cups, and others had to thread between them to get back into the building. There was a lot of daft behaviour and fun in the summer. When we came back in the autumn, we all had new clothes and new bags. We rehearsed a performance of *Hamlet* and Elena and I sat quietly enough to receive barely-speaking parts. For Christmas there was a real tree, fluffy with brown needles, drooping with glass balls and leaning sideways, in the corner of the main hall, and some of the girls wore bits of tinsel in their earrings.

We used to meet up at The Shakespeare pub most Friday nights. It was a vacillating, eager-to-please sort of pub, decorated with Irish-style trinkets and olde-worlde mismatched chairs, a Victorian ornate carpet and a real fire that was never lit. Widescreen TVs and big plastic speakers had been bolted in, and there was a slot machine flashing fruit and dollar signs and occasionally warbling to itself. The landlord seemed to have the idea that if we called ourselves students then we must be old enough to drink. I caught the bus into town from the caravan site and met up with Charlotte at the bus station; Elena and Lucy lived close enough to town to walk in together, sometimes arriving with some of the boys. We sent each other unnecessary texts. In the pub we re-arranged chairs and bought rounds and opened out bags of crisps so everyone could share. Elena flicked her hair and rolled her eyes and made everyone laugh; Charlotte was beautiful; Lucy was awkward and sometimes said too much, too loudly. Sometimes Fay and Ella came along; sometimes Joe came over to tease Elena; and sometimes all the boys - Joe, Ed, Kez and Ben - would come over and squeeze into seats between us and eat our crisps.

In our second year of college everyone was turning eighteen, and we spent a lot of time planning parties, or talking about parties that were imminent, or remembering parties that had been and gone. Everyone wanted their party to be at a nightclub or bar, but most had to settle for their parents 'house, imploring their parents to practise invisibility or even go out for the evening. The anticipation before a party and the gossip afterwards were as satisfying as the party itself. I didn't have one; Elena pressed me to throw one at her house, but I decided instead to have a Chinese meal, just the four of us, drinking wine and giggling. Elena was the last of us to turn eighteen, and although she spent most of the year planning her party she was worried that no-one would come.

"Everyone will have gone away," she said, twirling her fingers in her hair earnestly. "Once the exams are over everyone will be off to jobs. Or holidays. Or gap year stuff."

"Everyone will be ready for a party," disagreed Charlotte. "It'll be perfect timing. We'll have finished our exams; your party will be the ultimate end of term party."

"We could combine it!" exclaimed Lucy. "It could be a birthday party and an end of term party in one!"

Elena pulled a face.

"We wouldn't call it an end of term party," said Charlotte. "I just meant that everyone will be in the mood for your birthday."

Elena was not to be reassured. She put her hands to her face and groaned. "Oh, why do we make so much of our eighteenth? Why is it so special?"

"Too much pressure for it to be perfect," agreed Charlotte.

"What's so great about turning eighteen, anyway?" Elena went on. "I mean, it's supposed to be this great moment when you become an adult, but nothing really changes, does it?"

"You can drink legally," grinned Charlotte. We were sitting in The Shakespeare at the time, at our favourite table, drinking vodka

163

and orange, the bright liquid distorted through big bulbous ice cubes when I looked down into my glass.

"Oh, but it's not as much fun when it's legal!" cried Elena, and we all laughed and agreed. "Anyway," she went on, "turning eighteen doesn't mean anything real, does it? You're still living at home, still going to college, still got no money..."

"You can vote in elections," I pointed out.

"Big deal!"

"You're right," said Charlotte. "I don't feel any different now I'm eighteen; there's nothing different about my life. I'm still doing homework and asking my mum for money."

Elena grinned. "You could marry Kezza now if you want..."

Charlotte squealed and we all pretended not to look over at the table where the boys were sitting.

When we weren't talking about parties we were mostly groaning about coursework and revision for our final exams. Elena had drawn up a revision timetable: she had carefully allocated sections of days of the week to different subjects, with blocks of colour and regular meals and breaks scheduled. I could picture her at the desk in her bedroom, under her warm lamp and her cat pictures, the room perfumed with jasmine or rosemary from the scented candles twinkling on her bookshelf. Her mum brought her cups of tea and biscuits when she was studying. I had been to Lucy's house, too, and I knew that she liked to play music while she worked; and Charlotte liked to pile cushions on the floor and lay in a nest with her books and laptop. Charlotte had given me an embroidered cushion for my birthday, and when I studied at home, sitting on my bed, I propped up the cushion between my elbow and the smooth, cold wall of the caravan.

On rainy days, the caravan was dark inside, and I had the light on in my room even though dusk was still an hour away. The rain played steadily against my window. I was revising for my English exam, writing out and memorising some quotes that I hoped would be useful whatever the question. "There is nothing either good or bad, but thinking makes it so."

I didn't hear my mum come in. At that time she was working in a gift shop, but she finished at five so she must have gone somewhere else afterwards; I had assumed she was shopping, or meeting a friend, or maybe meeting a man, although she hadn't told me she was seeing anyone. I usually heard her when she came in because the whole caravan wobbled when the front door was opened or closed, but perhaps on this occasion I was too absorbed in what I was reading to notice. Usually, she would have called hello to me when she came in: the light was on in my room because of the rain, so she knew I was home. But this time I didn't hear her come in, and she didn't call, so the first moment I became aware of her was when my bedroom door swung open violently.

"I don't know how you've got the nerve," she spat, "to just sit there."

She looked terrifying. Her hair was dark and dripping from the rain, and her shiny, wet coat made her seem bigger than she was. Her eyes were enormous, enormous white and enormous black. She looked like a snarling dog.

"What?"

It was as if she had brought in something dark from outside: my room had been cosy and brightly lit, the bed dappled with books and notes, my pen in my hand and writing pad on my lap, my handwriting friendly and familiar, the rounded squiggles and the quick scribbling out... and she stood in my room, now, dark and wet and trembling with an unimagined, unexplained fury.

"I can't believe it, I can't believe what a bitch you are, a cold, calculating bitch... all these years..." She was choking on her words and she stopped and swallowed, shaking her head. "I thought you were the one person who would never turn against me, never let me down, never stab me in the back."

"I don't know what you're talking about!"

"I went to see Mark." She was actually trembling, a spasm running down her arms from her shoulders, and her voice sounded like it was trying to fight its way out of her throat so it could spring at me. It was frightening. "I rang him up and I went to see him. I thought, I thought there might be another chance for us. But he told me about you. He told me how you came on to him - what was it, a year ago, maybe two years? You were all over him, trying to snog him. You threw yourself at him."

Mark would never have said it like that. He wouldn't have used those words. He wouldn't have made it sound so ugly and coarse. He would have told her gently, out of concern, a sense of propriety, a belief in honesty. I felt hot embarrassment riding up my neck.

"How could you do that, you little bitch! You conniving, lying, sneaky little slut!"

I just sat there, too surprised to speak.

I had chosen not to remember the day when I went to Mark's and made a fool of myself. Just as there are places and experiences that I have carefully packed and labelled in my memory, there are places and experiences that I have torn up and thrown away. Some things are best unremembered.

"It wasn't like that," I said.

My voice was calm, and that ignited my mother. "Bitch!" she screamed, and snatched at the books on my bed. I shrank up to the pillow, my knees under my chin, and everything jumped in the air and fell about the tiny room.

"You lying bitch! You've ruined my life! You've always ruined my life!" She was trying to pick up my laptop, but her face was red and she was fumbling as if she could barely control her limbs. I pressed myself back against the wall. "Evil bitch!" She threw the laptop, and it cracked heavily against the door and thudded on the floor.

"It wasn't like that!"

What was it like? I had tried so hard not to remember. Time had passed and I had believed there were no traces of it left. Mark had been kind, and very grown up; I felt unbearably foolish. It was silly. I had gone to his house in a fit of - what? Loneliness? Yearning? Did I have a crush on him or his house? I had said silly things and immediately regretted them. He had let me back out of the situation and implied that we would both forget it had ever happened. Surely no-one should be held accountable for things they have disowned?

She stamped out of the room, shaking the whole caravan, and I heard her slamming about in the kitchen. I jumped lightly off the bed, barefoot, and stepped over the laptop in the doorway. My mother was lurching about like a drunk, but she had yanked open

166

the cutlery drawer and she drew out the big kitchen knife as if it was treasure she had dug for.

"I'll kill you!" she shouted. "I'll kill you and I'll kill him! The two of you, laughing at me, laughing at me behind my back..."

The front door of the caravan was between us, and I moved nimbly out of it. The rain was cold and the grating of the metal steps was sharp beneath my bare feet. As I ran onto the soft, mushy grass, I saw Barbara in the yellow light of her doorway. "Are you alright, dear?" she called. She was just in time to see my mother in the doorway of our caravan, with a big knife in her hand, yelling my name.

She calmed down. When she saw Barbara, she stopped yelling.

"Fucking hell," she muttered, shaking her head as it she needed to reset herself. Then she held the knife up, exhibiting it, both arms held out as if she was surrendering in the spotlight of a police helicopter, and then she tossed the knife as far as she could, away to the side, where it tumbled in the grass.

"I didn't mean it," she called out, steadily. "I'm just being an idiot. Overdramatic." She looked towards Barbara. "You can go in; nothing to see here." I heard Barbara's door bang shut. "Silly cow."

We stood in the rain, looking at each other. Although I was barefoot, I was dressed: I wore jeans and a shirt. I could feel my clothes becoming wetter, a cold weight on my head and shoulders and thighs. I watched her. She ran her hand across her eyes, and with the tips of her fingers she pinched the bridge of her nose in an intense, resolved gesture. She looked at me again.

"Okay," she said. "I shouldn't have gone off at the deep end like that."

She was far enough away that she had to call out to me, lifting her voice a little, like tossing a beanbag. "That was wrong of me, over reacting. I didn't mean all that. You're my daughter and I love you."

Her hair, I could see, even at this distance, was drenched, and it lay very dark and very flat against her head. She looked like stray animal. She shrugged and looked wearily downwards.

"I'm such a mess," she said, almost to herself.

"I'm sorry," I called. "I'm sorry about what happened with Mark. It was a silly thing. I don't know what came over me. It was... it was a moment of madness. That was why I never told you. I wanted to pretend it had never happened. It didn't mean anything."

She had looked up when I started to speak, and had been looking across at me, intensely. When I finished she continued to stare at me for a few seconds before responding.

"I think you probably wanted to hurt me," she called through the rain.

"No, of course not," I called back.

I had been lonely and miserable, back then. It was just before I started college. Perhaps I had just wanted a family, in some oblique way; I wanted Mark and his house and his ordinary life.

That was what I believed then, but now I'm not so sure that my mother wasn't right. Perhaps I did want to hurt her. Perhaps I wanted to show her that Mark wouldn't always be there for her. Perhaps I wanted to show her that he was too good for her. Perhaps I wanted to show her that I wouldn't always be there for her either, and that Mark and I were comrades, kindred spirits, people who understood each other and didn't need her. Perhaps I wanted her to see Mark and me ride off into the sunset together.

"I'm sorry I haven't been a better mother," she called. "I know it's been a wild ride."

"It's okay," I said.

"What?"

"I said, it's okay."

The rain fell. She rubbed her face tiredly with one hand.

"I just wish you hadn't fucked things up with me for Mark," she called. "You don't understand, but there's a real connection between us. You couldn't understand that."

She was claiming Mark as hers, not mine.

It was at that moment that she noticed something over my shoulder, and stared. I turned. It was a police car, bumping slowly and quietly over the grass towards us. I guessed Barbara had called them. The sirens weren't sounding but the lights were twirling, bright as a child's toy in the grey rain. It drove right up to us and stopped, the handbrake grinding, allowing two officers to jump

168

out. The one nearest to me was holding his hat in his hand, and I remember his graceful and proficient movement as he swung it up on to his head and said to me: "Are you alright?"

"No," I said. "She tried to kill me. That's the knife over there."

After she had been taken away, I told them everything. Everything and more. I told them she had been in a psychiatric hospital before, after she had threatened her ex-boyfriend with a knife. I told them she had sent him letters threatening to kill him and the police had been involved. I told them that she shoplifted compulsively and couldn't keep a job for more than a month. I told them that when I was a little girl, she smashed the walls of our house with a hammer in a furious fit of violence, and then deliberately set fire to the house, while we were still in it.

I took control of my life. All those magazines talk about taking control of your life, putting yourself first, finding inner strength, taking the first step on a journey to a new life. I took control: I swung upwards by swinging my mother down.

I agreed that I didn't want her to be prosecuted in court, but they told me they could hold her under some provision of the Mental Health Act, and she wouldn't be released until she had submitted to treatment. I remembered that there was a secure ward at the hospital, Chestnut Ward, and thought of her there, locked in with the other patients. I didn't try to visit her. Everyone I spoke to - police officers, social workers, psychiatric nurses - was very calm and concerned and professional, and I was very calm and concerned and mature back at them. Every minute of every day I felt heightened, concentrated. It was like being in a film.

I received a formal letter from the legal department of the hospital, and while I was marvelling that the hospital had a legal department I realised that the letter was telling me that I had the right, as next of kin, to appeal against my mother's sectioning under the Mental Health Act. She was in a Kafkaesque nightmare, whereby her right of appeal was offered to her accuser. I put the letter away.

My friends were in awe. Their parents sent me homemade food in tupperware, to heat up in the microwave. When I went to Elena's house for tea her mother gave me a hug.

169

And it turned out that Elena was wrong when she said that being eighteen didn't mean anything. Being eighteen means everything. At eighteen you can have your mother sectioned, and authorise doctors to administer drugs to keep her quiet. At eighteen you can be her next of kin and make her decisions for her. At eighteen you can access all the money your father put in trust for you; at eighteen you can draw out every penny, and find a flat to rent, and look for a job. At eighteen you can take control of your life, even at the expense of someone else's.

There was one night, before I moved out of the caravan, when I stopped for a moment. It was as if I had been rushing forwards along a fast road, looking only at the horizon ahead while the scenery on either side changed as rapidly as a kaleidoscope, and when I suddenly paused, the scene around me coalesced, and I saw where I was. I was alone in our caravan. It's funny, because at that moment it felt just as if she had died, as if a stroke or heart attack or accident had taken her very suddenly and brutally. All around me I saw our familiar plates and mugs, the kettle and the scratched frying pan, her shoes kicked into a corner, our magazines in a thick pile on the floor, and me on my own, watching the television, watching the programmes that just two weeks before we had been watching together, never suspecting that everything was about to end, forever, abruptly. It was as if something terrible had happened, something catastrophic and irreversible. A terrible mistake. I was afraid, and I wanted to ring them up and take it all back, but I knew it was too late.

The feeling passed. I got up and went on rushing forwards, eyes on the horizon, with no turning back.

Saturday

The sunlight made the street glitter, and even this far inland it felt like the seaside. People were out, smiling, walking dogs and children, but the road was quiet: no-one was going to work. When I arrived at the hospital car park, at my usual time, it was lazy and peaceful, with no queue and a generous scattering of spaces, as if everyone was still in bed.

I locked the car and looked up at my mother's window, dark in the shadow of the building. I had worn trousers today and felt more comfortable than in the swishy skirt of the day before. In the lobby of the hospital there were few people and a weekend atmosphere; the man behind the desk had his sleeves rolled up and was joking into the telephone. The kiosk was closed.

I followed my coloured line like a little toy train, buzzed into the ward, rubbing disinfectant gel into my hands, and walked down the corridor to my mother's room. She was wearing pink today, and lying quite flat, submerged in the bed. The morphine dispenser was swaddled in the sheets beside her, breathing its slow mechanical breaths. Before I sat down I crossed to open the window on the blue sky. The air bubbled in from outside, fresh and clear.

I sat down and watched her.

There were different nurses working today. A tall nurse with pointed elbows came in and said "Good morning" in a quiet voice, without looking at me. She fussed around my mother, tucking and adjusting, ripping open a mouth moistener and using it sharply. She went to the sink to wash her hands and the tap gushed over-excitedly into the tiny basin, splashing the nurse. She snatched at the tap and cut it short. She shook her hands in disgust and flicked at her clothes, then in turning caught my eye, nodded to me, and left.

I waited until almost ten o' clock before I went for a drink. It was already a day for sweating, so I chose a plastic bottle of apple juice instead of tea. It was sweet and sticky, and I drank it too quickly, giving myself no excuse to sit any longer in the canteen. The canteen was quiet at weekends too, with a grille over one of the hatches; instead of waiting in a queue, I had had to cough for attention until a woman came from the back to attend to the till, still smiling at someone's joke as she came. After toying with the empty juice bottle for a while, I walked back to my mother's ward along a corridor bleached by sunlight. A young man was walking gingerly with crutches while his girlfriend chattered at him.

When I got back to my mother's room the tall nurse was already in there, rummaging among the boxes on the shelf above the sink. She saw me and nodded mutely, then became more frantic in her rummaging, her pointed elbows snapping in and out and her hands snatching at slippery plastic packages. I don't know which of us was the intruder and which was intruded upon. In the end she clicked her tongue impatiently and gathered up all the boxes, a whole stack of different sizes, and left with them tucked under her chin.

I sat down. Even with the window open and the sun turned away, the room was warm. I heard the horn of a car in the car park below, but it sounded more like a greeting than a threat. Footsteps passed in the corridor, voices in conversation, a trundling trolley.

She died. It happened. I was sitting there and all of a sudden she didn't breathe. I stared. Then she did breathe, a long slow breath in, and a long slow breath out. Then there was silence again.

I waited. She didn't breathe. She didn't move. She didn't look any different. Nothing happened.

Was she dead? There was no clear moment of death, no event, no gasp or shudder. I sat in her limbo, watching her, listening for breaths. Time passed. She didn't breathe.

I wondered if I should call a nurse. It seemed obtuse to shout for help at the very moment when nothing could be done, but death was surely a crisis that should be attended to. I needed a nurse to come running: a witness, perhaps, or a judge, to determine death. An usher.

172

I went to the door and looked into the empty corridor. I looked back at my mother, but she looked the same. I had to walk down to the nurses 'station. "Please could you come..."

Two nurses came: the tall one and another woman, middle aged, with a lumpy, worried sort of face. The tall one held my mother's wrist and I stood waiting for a verdict. They communicated with each other by nods and grimaces.

"Is she dead?" I asked, and felt ashamed.

The tall nurse nodded. "She's gone," she said, and checked the time. "We'll give you a few minutes."

They left discreetly, and I stood, not sure what I was supposed to do. Outside, I could hear voices in the car park in the sunshine: people carrying on with their lives, chatting and laughing. She was dead. All that time spent dying was just leading up to this: nothing. All done. I sat down again but felt suddenly that the chair wasn't mine any more.

I waited for the nurses. At last they came back and started filling in a form and removing the morphine machine. They told me I would have to come back to the hospital on Monday to collect the death certificate because the office wasn't open at weekends. They gave me directions to the office for Monday. They gave me a card bearing the name of the hospital chaplain. I got up and they said goodbye sympathetically. I walked out into the corridor. This room felt like her room, where I came to visit her, but of course it wasn't; she wouldn't be there any more.

Although I hadn't seen her for so many years, I realised that she had continued to be an enormous presence in my life; or maybe an enormous absence; either way, she had now become a void. I walked down the corridor, past the nurses 'station and out of Marlowe Ward. I wondered whether to go to the canteen for lunch, but I had no reason to go there, perhaps no longer any right to go there. I should probably go home.

It was all over.

About the Author

Having worked for ten years as a criminal defence lawyer in busy courts and police stations, Sarah Healey settled down in the far reaches of West Cornwall to live a quiet life, writing and editing books.

She is the author of five novels: Red Blue Green, Having Fun, The Day of the Trial, The Night Watch, and A Week in the Life of Amelia Nash.

She also edits fiction and non-fiction and can be found at **sarahhealeyeditor.com**

www.ingramcontent.com/pod-product-compliance
Ingram Content Group UK Ltd.
Pitfield, Milton Keynes, MK11 3LW, UK
UKHW020644300625
6642UKWH00047B/1135

9 781915 975164